DISRUPTION LEADERSHIP MATTERS

Lessons for Leaders from the Pandemic

Gary Ryan

Published by Inspire Publishing 2021

First Edition 2021

Copyright © 2021 Gary Ryan

All rights reserved. No part of this publication may be reproduced, stored in a retrieval system, or transmitted in any form or by any means, electronic, mechanical, photocopying, recording or otherwise, without the prior written permission from both the copyright owner and publisher.

Disclaimer:
All the information, techniques, skills, and concepts contained within this publication are of the nature of general comment only and are not in any way recommended as individual advice. The intent is to offer a variety of information to provide a wider range of choices now and in the future, recognising that we all have widely diverse circumstances and viewpoints. Should any reader choose to use the information contained herein, this is their decision. The author and publishers do not assume any responsibility whatsoever under any condition or circumstance.

Images for Figures, 1, 7 and 9 were purchased from Getty Images.

Book design & layout : Surendra Gupta

ISBN: 978-1-922618-54-2 (pbk – hard cover)
ISBN: 978-1-922618-53-5 (pbk)
ISBN: 978-1-922618-55-9 (e-book)

Visit: www.disruptionleadershipmatters.com

To Michelle, Liam, Sienna, Callum, Aiden, and Darcy. I love each of you past the moon, the stars, the sun, and back again. The way each of you has managed your battles with our crazy world over the past two years inspires me every day, more than each of you realise. Every time we say goodbye, never forget my words, "I luv ya and miss ya."

Foreword

I've journeyed with Gary Ryan for more than 11 years now, sharing our thoughts and insights on leadership and the challenges and excitement of our work. There's something quite empowering about travelling with someone whose ideas and insights spark off something within you that develops and enhances your learning. Such has been my experience with Gary.

In our leadership development work, our workshops, coaching and mentoring of leaders, we've both talked about "disruption" for many years. However, neither of us had contemplated the enormous impact of the COVID disruption on our world, country, organisations, and professional and personal lives. Nor were we ready for the suddenness upon which it descended, not to mention its intransigence about leaving!

Back in early 2020, as it became evident that this "virus" was taking hold and beginning to disrupt our lives in an unprecedented way, Gary and I began to have long Zoom calls about how we could support the leaders who looked to us for inspiration and motivation. Some of those we had worked with were pivoting rapidly, refocusing their leadership style, and recreating their organisations as a result. Other leaders were very challenged, unable to see a way through, watching COVID not only disrupt what they had created but also make it seemingly irrelevant.

Those leaders struggled with knowing how to lead their people through this unpredictable time, fearing for the future of their organisation.

Many of our leadership development programs and workshops were cancelled or postponed as lockdowns came into force. Our coaching and mentoring continued, but only the proactive leaders recognised that more than at any other time, this was a financial investment they needed to make in their leadership development right now if they were to lead and support their people through this pandemic. Our concern was for the others who could not see a way through. It became apparent that it was time to write a book, and we had time to do it, and Gary has led the way.

Gary is a highly experienced leadership development coach and workshop facilitator. He is regularly contracted to present his business and leadership development programs within university departments. He has worked with CEOs and senior leaders not only here in Australia but globally. While academically highly educated in his field and therefore theoretically grounded, he is sought after by organisations because his leadership development programs are very practical. He is known for his ability to provide the psychological safety leaders need to talk about, the actual day-to-day challenges they face. He then can provide strategies, insights, and skill development to assist those leaders in meeting those challenges when they return to the office. He meets people where they are and tailors his work to the specific needs of each leader and the organisation.

As Gary says, Disruption Leadership Matters – Lessons for Leaders from the Pandemic is a book about "leadership in action."

It challenges leaders to refocus their leadership thinking. In many cases, they unlearn how they did leadership for years before this pandemic and relearn new ways to develop and enhance their leadership style to meet this new normal.

For Gary, this is about leaders putting people first and enabling them to be the best they can be for themselves and the organisation. The leaders who quickly pivoted as COVID-19 descended were those who recognised at the outset that they didn't have all the answers. They didn't know what to do, so they led from the centre, not from the top, and brought their people into a collaborative process of problem-solving, critical reflection and decision making, and they listened and learned. The result was a pooling of diverse talent, experience, expertise, and wisdom that saw them move to new ways of working with their people. As a result, they were 150% engaged in the process, while other leaders and organisations were stuck floundering, restricted by their pre-pandemic thinking. Therefore, his message to leaders in this book is that if they want to move confidently and proactively into a new future, they need to engage their people and lead differently.

His eight chapters show how leaders can do that. It's a book to be studied either alone or with your team. It shows you a road through, and if you find great value in Gary's insights, you will find yourself thinking: "If I have gained this much from his book, how much more might I gain from working with him?"

Disruption will be a constant presence in the lives of leaders into the foreseeable future. There will be no going back to the way things used to be, to lead the way they did before. While this book is about leading through this current pandemic, its message will empower leaders with the skills and mindsets they need to

navigate the next disruption and the one after that, as unpredict-
ability and uncertainty become the new normal.

Gary's book has the potential to be your roadmap through to
this new normal. I highly recommend you read it.

Maree Harris, PhD
Director, People Empowered
https://peopleempowered.com.au

Contents

Foreword v

Introduction 1

The structure of the book 8

Chapter One: Engagement matters 13

Is employee engagement the sole responsibility
of leaders? 17

Demonstrating the ease with which leaders can
drive down employee engagement 19

How to maintain engagement under extreme
circumstances 25

Chapter Two: Start by assessing your mental models 30

Unconscious bias, diversity, and inclusion 35

The knowing-doing gap..40

Push through the learning curve 42

Words matter 47

The leader-learner trap 50

Mental models to consider 53

    Employees are human beings, not human resources 53

    Learning and oxygen are equally crucial for
    human beings 54

    Smart, hard work 55

    Cash is king. Clarity is queen. 59

    Whoever receives the output of your work so that
    they can do their work is a customer 61

    Take responsibility and own your role, versus blame
    and excuses 62

Chapter Three: The triune brain 65

    Mental health, wellbeing, and leadership 69

        Mindfulness matters 71

Chapter Four: Triple empathy, connection, and
               role clarity 74

    Triple empathy 75

    Triple connection 77

    Triple role clarity 83

Can I do this if we don't have a consistent approach
to leadership across the organisation? 86

Chapter Five: Vision matters! 90

Roadblocks help you to recognise your vision is missing 95

Use the disruption to revisit your vision...97

How to overcome the frustration that comes
with a vision...98

Chapter Six: The quality of your conversations matters 100

High-quality conversation characteristics....................................105

Chapter Seven: Don't just read - take action! 119

How to seek regular feedback from colleagues............................121

A structure for face-to-face feedback 122

Chapter Eight: Moving beyond the pandemic................................126

Acknowledgements 137

Bibliography & Resources 139

About the Author 143

Introduction

n 2007, I founded Organisations That Matter promoting people within organisations as human beings, not "human resources." A fair day's pay, for a fair day's work, where people could go home free from concerns about work, always seemed to make sense to me. After all, these people are more likely to have happier homes and are more likely to be better contributors to their community. Call it an algorithm, if you will, but it is a formula that can work for the good of all.

In 1995, I was introduced to Robert K Greenleaf's work on Servant Leadership. As the ninth child in a family of 11 children (I am also a twin), the concept and practices of Servant Leadership resonated with me; it matched my experience of my upbringing. My parents, Eddie and Olga Ryan, were true servant leaders.

I had the good fortune of meeting Jack Lowe at the first Servant Leadership conference in Australia in October 1999, and Jack became a mentor for many years. Jack was the CEO of TD Industries, a company in the early years of an uninterrupted 20-year reign as one of the Fortune 100 Best Employers in the USA. In late 2000, I watched a video of a speech by Dee Hock, CEO Emeritus of VISA International, given at the 2000 Greenleaf Centre For Servant Leadership 10th Annual Conference. Jack introduced Dee to the audience as Dee was a practitioner of

Servant Leadership after being introduced to Robert Greenleaf's work in 1971.

Among many profound statements in Dee's speech, one struck a chord with me. It seemed to resonate with my DNA. *"People are not "things" to be manipulated, labelled, boxed, bought, and sold. Above all else, they are not "human resources" They are entire human beings, containing the whole of the evolving universe, limitless until we start limiting them. We must examine the concept of leading and following with new eyes. We must examine the concept of superior and subordinate with increasing scepticism. We must examine the concept of management and labor with new beliefs. And we must examine the nature of organizations that demand such distinctions with an entirely different consciousness. It is true leadership; leadership by everyone; leadership in, up, around, and down this world so badly needs, and dominator management it so sadly gets."*

Dee, the founder of the world's most successful financial institution, said that human beings are not human resources! I commenced a Graduate Diploma in Human Resource Management in July 1999 and studied part-time via distance education because I worked full-time. I had expected that the course would be about people. People were constantly referenced as "resources" and "subordinates" or "assets" and "capital." I struggled with what I had been learning because it seemed at odds with my core beliefs and values. But I could not describe my struggle. I could not explain it and put it into words. Then, listening to Dee, the words I had struggled to find to describe my challenges with the course exploded from the screen. At its essence, I did not believe that people were resources. What a profound insight. That is what I do not like about the course! People are NOT resources! Despite my dissonance, I struggled through and completed the degree in 2003. I needed the qualification for my career. Fortunately, my Master of Management was a completely different experience. I am forever grateful to the fantastic team of academics from Monash University and Swinburne University who delivered such a life-changing course.

When I formed Organisations That Matter, I wanted to make a difference and help leaders treat people as human beings. The research was overwhelming. People who fully use their talents in the service of their organisation, and ultimately their clients, customers, and stakeholders, are more engaged. More engaged people give more discretionary effort, which increases productivity. Treating people as human beings is great for the bottom line. Yet, my experience was that very few leaders treated people as human beings. Instead, they treated them as resources, capital, or assets. They could be manipulated, coerced, labelled, boxed, and figuratively bought or sold or, worse, thrown out with the garbage.

There is another, more profound benefit to treating people as human beings when they are at work. They go home less stressed, and the issues they face at work are less likely to intrude on their personal life. They have the right not to have work negatively affect their home life. When their work creates less stress, they can be more "present" at home and have better family lives. Better family or home lives lead to better communities, and everyone benefits. Leadership is a heavy burden, but the rewards can be exponential, as can be the downside to poor leadership.

Since 2007, I have worked with many terrific leaders in organisations on the journey of transition from a human resource perspective to one where people are seen as human beings.

This transition is not easy, nor is it linear. A rear-guard reaction inevitably occurs, and the industrial age views that people are resources kicks in, stronger than ever. Despite this, my passion for helping organisations be great for followers, leaders, and the organisations themselves, has never waned. The late Robert Ackoff, Professor Emeritus of the Wharton Business School, said it best: *"Ages don't stop and start. One fades in, while the other fades away."* Each time a rear-guard industrial age response has occurred in the shift to seeing people as human beings, I've regarded it as a consequence of fading ages – it is never a smooth process and is likely to exceed my lifetime.

Then, seemingly out of nowhere, the COVID-19 pandemic spread across the world. The economic impact was bound to surface what leaders in governments and organisations *really* think about the people they lead. Given the propensity of the virus to kill older people, I was amazed at how many conversations were taking place that included an *"acceptable death toll, so long as we can keep the economy going."* Huge numbers of staff were stood down within a matter of days of isolation measures commencing. There were very few conversations about engaging with employees to determine a sustainable financial solution. Instead, people were consigned to the financial scrapheap, left to fend for themselves, despite the virus being no fault of their own. I appreciate that no one asked for the pandemic, and very few saw it coming. I understand that we all exist within an economic reality, and numbers do matter. But here we were, treating human beings as if they were numbers. Nothing more, nothing less.

The unfolding of the pandemic got me thinking. Maybe, the pandemic could provide the disruption that leaders needed to re-consider "how" they lead. Perhaps the pandemic would be the catalyst for reflection that helped leaders see the pre-existing flaws in their leadership and thinking to which they were blind? What if leaders within the HR industry paused to reflect on what the acronym "HR" actually means? What if they chose to change the name to something more people-focused due to that reflection? What if people with "HR" in their title decided to have a conversation about the name of their role? I witnessed leaders taking actions that they seemed to dislike but were compelled to do because that is *what a leader must do*. These leaders appeared helplessly trapped in a failing, 20th-century mindset, yet they could not see any other way of being a leader.

Indeed, there must exist other examples where leaders had shown that human beings do matter. Despite the harsh reality of the numbers, a genuinely humanistic version of leadership was likely occurring while other leaders defaulted to the "humans as resources" view of the world. What if I found and shared examples that showed that the leaders could care for their people and manage the numbers simultaneously? What if there were lessons that could prepare organisations for the downtimes when applied during the "good times?" After all, Bob Chapman, CEO of Barry Wehmiller, a company with a US$3 billion turnover and employs 12,000 staff across the world, says, *"Economies do not follow a straight line. They go up and down. It is my responsibility to build a business model that can sustain the downs."*

And so, I wanted to write this book. I wanted to provide leaders with an opportunity to see the world through a different lens. While enormous pain has been inflicted upon economies, and I wish it had not occurred, what if there was a resource that could help leaders become true leaders of human beings? What if this disruption could have a positive outcome? What if the disruption could increase the speed at which we move away from industrial age thinking and behaving? What if there was a resource that could show you how to lead in the 21st century? So, I started writing. I was encouraged on the day I started writing by a LinkedIn post by one of my peers, Maree Harris:

"The worst thing we ever did in corporate America (and Australia?) was to take the most vital part of any company - the people powering it - and label it so dismissively as 'human resources'." Such an important comment to be made by Adriana Stan and Tom Goodwin in this World Economic Forum article on where HR is at and where it needs to be. We all mouth those words "our people are our greatest assets", but they are too often treated as mere "resources" and when people are treated like that they tend to become an organisations' greatest liability."

Maree and I had met at a facilitator workshop organised by Ian Berry in 2010. We struck up a friendship and have remained in contact over the past 11 years. Maree's post was the confirmation I needed. Write the book!

I live with my wife and five children in Melbourne, Australia. Between 2020 and 2021, Melbourne has been the most locked down city in the world. I have written the manuscript during this period, and as of October 2021, when the final draft is about to be sent to the editor, we continue to be in lockdown. I am incredibly proud of Michelle and our five children, Liam, Sienna, Callum, Aiden, and Darcy. We have been fortunate that COVID-19 is yet to enter our humble home. While comfortable, not all children have a bedroom to themselves. One of our children, Callum, is an elite dancer, and the family agreed for him to use the living area for his classes, despite this area being the heart of the house. Our children have remained responsible for their learning from tertiary level to primary school. Michelle has been extraordinary with her work, set up in our walk-in wardrobe in our bedroom. I have continued to operate the business, which was negatively impacted by the first lockdown in 2020. I am forever grateful to my clients, many of whom I have worked with over multiple years, for their loyalty and support during these difficult times.

Together we have experienced too many lockdown birthdays to count, non-COVID medical issues and surgery, brief moments of relief and excitement from the removal of restrictions, opportunities where we escaped from the city to spread our wings in the countryside, to our fair share of dark moments and many, many conversations about controlling what we can, and letting go, as best we can, what we can't. Our daughter, Sienna, turned 18 and completed her Year 12 education in 2020, and commenced her university degree this year. We were fortunate to have a 21st birthday party for our eldest son, Liam, albeit with restrictions on the number of guests. Both Michelle and I share responsibilities with our siblings for our elderly mothers.

From a leadership perspective, the most crucial test of our leadership has been with our family. I can promise that everything Michelle and I have learned over the years has been drawn upon to help us navigate this most extraordinary experience. Like what it did to your life, the pandemic has significantly impacted every aspect of our lives. I understand we are not unique, but we have certainly had **our** unique experience of the pandemic. We dream of regaining our freedoms and of the day when the pandemic is a memory. No doubt, you do, too. Please remain safe and healthy, and I hope you enjoy the book.

The structure of the book

The book is designed to provide concepts, theories, models, tools, and action items. I intend you to have an increased understanding of the thinking, theory, and logic that supports leadership in action.

Leadership can be outstanding for you, the leader, the people you lead, and your organisation's bottom line.

The more you understand the theories and concepts that support action, the more likely you will persist with an activity that gets results over time. The disruption caused by the global COVID-19 pandemic has caused us to re-think every aspect of our lives. For me, re-thinking leadership sits at the top of the list as we have seen the extraordinary power that resides in the hands of leaders of governments, industries, companies, religions, and, indeed, families.

My hope is this book will catalyse you to think about your beliefs and the actions and behaviours those beliefs drive. Various organisations, including global, domestic, for-profit, not-for-profit, schools, and governments, are featured throughout the book. I have witnessed many examples first-hand through my work, and I am grateful to the many leaders who have agreed for their stories to be included in the content. Everyone has been impacted by the pandemic, and leadership is relevant for all organisations of all shapes and sizes, so a broad range of organisational examples is included throughout the chapters. Some examples have required significant financial resources to enable them to be implemented. Many other examples highlight seemingly small efforts. In sport, these examples are called "one percenters." The small things matter and add up over time. These examples show you that throughout the disruption and in so-called "normal" times, effective leadership is achieved through the culmination of many small efforts.

In Chapter One, I focus on employee engagement and its relationship to productivity. I share a couple of negative examples of leadership that occurred early in 2020 that won't require you to read a survey result for you to identify that employee engagement would have been negatively affected by the behaviour of the leaders. From that point forward, I share many specific examples highlighting how leaders have taken action and led in a manner that emphasises the people in their organisations are human beings. These are the practical examples from which you can learn how to lead in the 21st Century.

Chapter Two asks you to consider your mental models about leadership and explains how this concept directly influences your behaviour as a leader. A range of recommended mental models is shared and described for your consideration. Chapter Three builds on these concepts and explains the Triune Brain theory from neuroscience. As a leader, your awareness of the function of the brain is essential for effective leadership, especially during unpredictable times.

Chapter Four provides three themes for working with the people in your organisation to assist with calming the emotional and irrational behaviours that may be triggered within the brains of the people you lead. Chapter Five re-enforces the power of vision and why it has never been more critical than now. Chapter Six explains the core skill that leaders require to navigate the disruption and beyond. This skill is worth investing time and effort in as you move forward to enable all the people in your organisation to better communicate with each other.

Chapter Seven outlines a process for conversational feedback. In the work I do, the courage to be able to provide candid feedback in a manner that is respectful and for the greater good of both the recipient and the organisation is the primary differentiator between an organisation that is moving toward a great culture and one that remains, at best, a good culture.

Chapter Eight, the final chapter, shares thoughts from select leaders about the future, the changes the disruption has caused that will last for the foreseeable future, what it means for their industry and what questions remain unanswered as we move to live beyond lockdowns.

You will notice that some people referenced in the text use the term HR manager. Some of them have started having conversations about the appropriateness of that term, and it doesn't mean that if you are an HR manager or lead a company that uses that term, you don't believe people are human beings. In some cases, they have recognised it is a 20th century term and might not be relevant for the 21st century. I'm not here to tell you what to do. Instead, I'm hopeful that the book catalyses conversations that might not otherwise occur. Do the words and labels you use reflect what you believe?

You will notice that I do not reference governments and political leaders. I would not have liked to have been in their shoes during these most difficult times, and I am not an epidemiologist. In democracies, the people will make their judgements at future elections. Over time, I suspect numerous academics will research and judge the performance of our political leaders. I will leave commentary of political leaders in their hands. That said, the lessons shared in the book are no doubt useful for all leaders, including those in government.

If you recognise that you are not as effective a leader as you would like, that is okay. Read on, and you will discover a plethora of clear, practical actions that will help you become the leader you wish to be. Ultimately, no book provides the answer to better leadership. You can't theorise your way to improvement. Instead, you must practice. You must take action. As you read this book and ideas for action pop into your mind, note them down and then act on them, as action is the key to improving your leadership.

Best wishes,

Gary Ryan
October 2021

Chapter One:
Engagement matters

As a leader, always ask yourself, *"Is what I am about to do likely to increase the engagement of our people or decrease it?"*

In the early 1990s, Sears-Roebuck completed a range of internal research projects. They wanted to know if there was a clear relationship between how satisfied an employee was with the organisation, and how that corresponded with customer satisfaction and how that, in turn, affected turnover. After several years, they identified a formula, what we would now call an algorithm.

As employee satisfaction scores rise by five points, customer satisfaction goes up by 1.3 points, and revenue goes up by 0.5 points. The 0.5 points increase in revenue should go straight to your bottom line if all else is equal. Who would not want that outcome? You do not have to be a "for profit" organisation to desire having engaged employees. Whether they be patients, students, clients, community members, etcetera, they will be better served by engaged employees versus disengaged employees. And it will free up valuable resources to enable you to serve your customers, community, and stakeholders better. The same is true if you are a not-for-profit organisation or government department, or agency. Highly engaged staff will better serve your stakeholders, be more productive and free valuable financial resources that could be used to provide more services.

Garry Ridge, CEO at WD40, is also an adjunct professor at the University of San Diego, where he has been teaching in a graduate leadership program for over 13 years. In his course, Garry shares research indicating that more than 70% of employees are not engaged with their organisation. Leading in a manner that enables employee engagement to be high makes sense. It is good for the employees, good for the leaders and good for the organisation. Given up to 70% of employees are disengaged, there is a massive opportunity for leaders to increase engagement. That leader could be you.

In her book, *Dare to Lead*, Brene Brown's research shows that humans are naturally wary creatures. In a professional context, imagine you hold a jar for every relationship. The jar contains marbles. Brene calls them "trust marbles." Each marble represents how much you trust the other person in your professional relationship. If the jar is packed to the brim with marbles, this will mean complete trust in your colleague. Very few jars are that full. How full do you believe a jar would be at the start of a professional relationship? Brene's research indicates that, on average, a professional relationship commences with the jar about 20% full.

Many people are surprised when I shared this information in workshops. It seems less than they expected. I then ask, "How do marbles get in the jar once a professional relationship commences?" After some conversation, a general agreement emerges. Trust marbles are added to the jar one at a time. In other words, trust is earned a little bit at a time.

On the other hand, when marbles come out of the jar, workshop attendees agree that they tend to come out in handfuls rather than one at a time. As the old saying goes, "Trust is hard to earn and easy to lose."

Consider your behaviour. What do you do that increases trust, and what is it that you do that decreases trust? Complete the table below. The left-hand column represents trust-building behaviours. The right-hand column represents trust-reducing behaviours.

Trust-building behaviours	Trust-reducing behaviours

Typical responses from the workshops I conduct include:

Trust-building behaviours	Trust-reducing behaviours
Follow through with what you say you will do – let people know ASAP if something happens that prevents you from following through	Saying one thing and doing another
Recognise people for their ideas and contribution	Claiming successes for yourself and being quick to blame others when things go wrong
Be honest and caring	Lie
Recognise people for their contributions	Claiming the work of others as your own
Listening	Not listening and constantly talking over the top of others
Displaying empathy	Lacking awareness of other people and what is going on in their life

From a leadership perspective, this is critical information. Leaders must be aware of how their actions either contribute to trust or detract from it. It is not hard to see the correlation between trust and engagement. Let us consider a high trust-building initiative that occurred at the start of the pandemic.

Thailand's Chareon Pokphand Group (CP Group) employs more than 400,000 people across 20 countries. Among other things, the company is one of the world's most extensive food and agro-businesses. On 3rd September 2020, CEO Supachai Chearavanont shared in an interview with Christine Tan, the host of CNBC's *Managing Asia* series, that the CP Group had a responsibility to protect employees from the pandemic. The group's leaders believed they had to ensure the continuing employment of their people and care for them through extra support if other family members, who did not work for CP Group, became unemployed due to the pandemic. Food vouchers were supplied to families where one of the parents had lost their job, even though that family member did not work for CP Group. When a CP Group service ceased operation due to economic forces, staff were re-deployed to other roles to maintain job security. To offset the cost of keeping people employed, Supachai Chearavanont challenged leaders within CP Group to find savings in non-human expenses to offset the cost of maintaining employees. The leaders' actions included reducing office space because the staff could work from home and transferring the savings from reduced travel costs to salary expenses. Think about that for a second. Instead of immediately looking at ways to reduce costs by reducing "headcount," CP Group focussed on reducing the cost of its physical resources to ensure it could continue to pay employees' salaries.

In a speech at the UN Global Impact Leaders Summit on 23rd June 2021, Supachai Chearavanont reinforced this message. He shared that CP Group was committed to hiring and promoting younger people, improving the diversity of the people in the organisation, and working with governments in private–public partnerships that had proved to be a successful model throughout the pandemic. CP Group's care for its employees is extraordinary, but is employee engagement the employer's sole responsibility?

Is employee engagement the sole responsibility of leaders?

The simple answer is a resounding no. Employees share a level of responsibility for their engagement. An employee is not a child in a parent–child relationship. It is not the leader's responsibility to "look after them." Employees are responsible for their role and performing it to the best of their ability. If they require help, they ought to seek it. If they need to learn something to perform their role, they ought to be willing learners. If they do not understand how to be successful in their position, they ought to have the courage to make suggestions and ask questions until they are clear about what they should be doing. If employees believe in the organisation's espoused values, they ought to be responsible for doing their best to behave consistently with those values, regardless of how their colleagues or leaders are acting.

In the workshops I facilitate, this topic has generated some fascinating conversations. Most participants indicate that they agree with the intention of their organisation's espoused values. Yet, they also share that they do not consciously behave according to them because they do not believe their leaders act consistently with the values, so why should they behave in such a way? I ask, "Do you believe in the stated values?" "Yes," is their response. "But I don't see the leader behaving that way, so why should I?"

This question is fair. It **is** far better when leaders act in a manner that is consistent with the organisation's values. However, if you believe in the values, why would you base your behaviour on someone you think is **NOT** acting consistently with them? The result is that you, too, end up behaving against your beliefs. Why would you do that to yourself? If you believe in the values, then take personal responsibility for acting consistently with them.

The speed at which employees pivoted to working from home on a global scale **shows** that employees take responsibility for their work and level of engagement. The effort that employees went to using their resources was extraordinary. What if 2020 had not experienced a global pandemic? Imagine if your organisation set up a project on 31st January 2020 with a goal for the organisation to have the capability for everyone to work from home by 31st December 2020. When you think of all the meetings, the cost of consultants, overcoming resistance from some staff, and the cost of providing the equipment so team members **could** work from home, what do you think the project's total cost would have been? I do not know the specific dollar amount, but I know it would have been a lot of money, time, and effort. And I am not sure the project would have been a success in every organisation.

On one level, I am not sure organisations worldwide could ever fully repay their staff for keeping their organisations going and doing it quickly and with little resistance in the early stages of the pandemic. In many examples, to this day, staff continue to pivot from the office to home, with little warning.

Having established that employees share responsibility for their level of engagement with their organisation, leaders profoundly influence an employee's experience. Let us explore two examples that demonstrate how easy it is for leaders to drive down employee engagement.

Demonstrating the ease with which leaders can drive down employee engagement

Often, it is not what leaders do to increase engagement. It is what they do to decrease it that matters. Organisations with espoused values and people-based cultures have not all passed the test. What leaders deeply believe to be true has been driven to the surface by the pandemic and is there for all to see. As a result of leaders behaving in alignment with their deep-seated mindsets, employees have withdrawn trust marbles by the handful. The following story is based on an example from a school in Australia.

Within three weeks of moving from on-site learning to remote learning in April 2020, the principal emailed 40 targeted teachers. The teachers were categorised as "under-allotted," meaning they had on-site commitments that could not be conducted online, such as inter-school sport and other specialist subjects.

The email informed the staff that within 36 hours, they were to book a meeting with the principal, deputy principal, and the human resources manager to discuss whether they would receive a reduction in salary commensurate with their "under-allotment" or what substitute work they could do to balance their load.

When receiving this late afternoon email, do you think the stress levels of those teachers went up, remained the same, or went down? Like everyone else in the world, the teachers were experiencing the commencement of a global pandemic which seemed, at the time, to have the potential to cause millions and millions of people to die. They had families to consider, including parents, siblings, friends, and for many of them, their partners, and children. What, do you believe, is the most likely stress response? We will come back to this point in a moment.

First, let us consider the concern regarding under-allotted teachers. On the surface, is it fair that under-allotted staff be allowed to remain under-allotted? After all, what about the fully allotted teachers who had 100% of their load transferred online? It would not be fair if these under-allotted staff got away with doing less work. Would it?

However, does merely looking at the timetable data tell the whole story? Purely data-driven leaders are not interested in the story behind the data. Instead, they rationalise their behaviour based on the data that is in front of them. For them, there is nothing else to consider. In this example, the timetable data indicated that the teachers were under-allotted, so something needs to be done about that. Either they receive less pay, or they do more work due to redeployment to other activities. Simple! Unfortunately, this response is a dangerous path to follow if you value human talent.

There is always a story behind the data. Without access to the story, leaders will miss a large piece of the employee engagement puzzle and make decisions that directly reduce engagement. If you would like to learn how to "see" the data behind a story, I encourage you to read Shawn Callahan's book, *Putting Stories to Work - Mastering Business Storytelling*. As a simple example, in 2001, when the Twin Towers were flown into by hijacked aircraft, the US Federal Aviation Administration (FAA) had to land 5,000 planes as quickly as possible. If you are a data person, you would be at risk of believing that the air traffic controllers followed their standard "rules" to land all 5,000 planes. However, never having completed a task like this in their history, air traffic controllers quickly recognised that their standard procedures would not be successful. Keep in mind that all 5,000 planes had to land **safely**, ensuring all on board were safe and well.

Instead of following the rules, air traffic controllers picked up the phone and called their colleagues, asking if they had any room for more planes to land. Based on these conversations, planes were allocated to airfields. The relationships between air traffic controllers proved to be more critical in such disruption than any rule book. Post-911, the FAA used the lesson to ensure that as more and more technology is introduced into aviation, the opportunity for air traffic controllers to develop relationships with their colleagues needs to be maintained and prioritised. This story's point is that an organisation's ability to respond to the unpredictable correlates with the strength of relationships between its people. Relationships, as it turns out, affect employee engagement. Better relationships equal increased engagement. And, as you have read, there is always a *story* behind the data.

The seminal Sears-Roebuck employee engagement research established the relationship between employee engagement and productivity. We know that engaged employees contribute more discretionary effort than disengaged employees, which in turn has a positive influence on productivity. It does not benefit any leader if their behaviour directly causes employees to become disengaged. Therefore, *striving to maintain engagement during unpredictable times ought to be an essential goal for leaders.*

At the school mentioned above, leaders ought to have first considered if the effort required to discover the stories behind the data was more important than doing **nothing**. In other words, was the risk that up to 40 staff were in fact "better off" than their colleagues after the move to online learning worth investigating, or could it be left on the shelf for a later date? Was investigating this issue worth the possible negative consequences it could cause? Was it worth investigating this issue "now" when remote learning was new to most schools, teachers, and students, and no one knew how long schools would have to operate online?

Think about it. Not even three weeks after successfully achieving the most dramatic change in the way education is delivered to students, a move that was only made due to the extraordinary effort of both administrators and teachers alike, the three most senior leaders at the school were going to conduct 40 staff meetings over three days. That is a considerable effort. If you have ever undertaken 40 sessions over three days, then you know how extraordinarily difficult that is to do with a consistent level of presence, empathy, and dialogue. However, if the exercise is about *looking* like you are engaging with your people, then you might be able to do it. Because deep listening, empathy, and dialogue will not be the tools you will be using during those meetings.

Of course, **while you are conducting these meetings, you are not doing anything else**. You are not considering what the first step away from online learning might look like and how you might prepare for it, and you're not looking at what life with all students back at school will look like either. What you are doing is putting an extraordinary effort into a problem that may only be in existence for several weeks. And you certainly aren't thinking about the impact of your behaviour on the mental health of the people you lead.

Leaders must have foresight, which is the ability to see how actions taken or not taken, will affect your desired future. Of course, there are multiple stories behind the data in this example. Each of the 40 teachers has their own story. I'm often reminded of a quote from Michelle Hunt, a one-time advisor to President Clinton in the USA, and founder of Dreammakers, *"Leadership is a serious meddling in other people's lives."* Imagine if, as a leader, you repeatedly asked yourself if the action you were considering taking was helping or meddling? If it is meddling, then do not do it.

From an economic perspective, it is difficult to understand the math. The time and effort by the senior leaders to conduct the investigation and deliver its outcomes while risking long-term damage to the engagement of their teachers are hard to calculate against any short-term gains that may have resulted from reducing the salary of some staff.

At the most senior level, what kind of conversations were taking place? What are the chances that anybody asked the question, "What might be some unintended consequences of going down this under-allotted path with our teachers?" This type of question, folks, is a fundamental question to ask when the action you are considering may result in disengaging staff.

A similar example occurred with the CEO of an energy provider. An email was sent to staff stating that if they had primary school-aged children being home-schooled, the staff member was required to use their leave because the CEO did not believe they could be productive. This directive was a command. Yet, staff who had primary school-aged children were already working productively from home and had already done what was necessary to set themselves up, mainly using their pre-existing home-based resources, to enable them to continue to work.

All it took was a global email from the CEO to cause hundreds, if not thousands, of trust marbles to be heard (metaphorically speaking) tumbling out of the employees' trust jars.

Most people's jobs cause them enough stress when they go home, without the behaviour of their leaders adding to their stress. It could be as simple as the leader was having a bad day, so they were abrupt with a colleague. Or they didn't listen or read a reply email correctly and jumped to a false conclusion and made a demand for work to be re-done at the end of the day when the staff member was about to go home. And the next day, they questioned why the work had been re-done when it didn't have to be because they had re-read the email in the morning and realised the work had been completed the previous afternoon.

Folks, I have witnessed this behaviour. It causes staff to go home more stressed than they need to be. And it is the leader's behaviour that catalyses this stress. When people go home stressed, it affects their home life and families. Do you, as a leader, have the right to do that? I don't believe you do, and hopefully, you don't, either. Therefore, leaders need to be acutely aware they are leading human beings. From this point forward, I share clear, concise examples of exactly how many leaders have led in a productive and humanistic manner throughout the pandemic.

How to maintain engagement under extreme circumstances

Nutrien Ag Solutions Australia (Nutrien) is the country's largest agricultural business. With more than 4,000 staff operating from 700 locations, 48% of the natural food served on dinner plates across the country comes directly from the services provided by the company. In his own words, Managing Director Rob Clayton says he is addicted to the success of the employees and agents associated with the business and the success of the farmers and communities they serve. Recently, profit-sharing opportunities were made available to employees. When Rob hears employees share stories about how their increased success has allowed them to buy their first new car, it delights him. The phrase, *"This is my business, and I'm serving my community,"* is precisely the mindset that Rob knows is essential for Nutrien to be able to demonstrate the big responsibility the company has in serving Australians.

When the pandemic caused the first lockdown in March 2020, Rob and his fellow leaders used a range of communication channels to remind staff that, as always, the company's biggest concern was the safety and well-being of staff and the community they serve. Given many frontline staff were permitted to work on-site due to their role, Rob was aware many of them were concerned for their safety. Their concerns were understandable, so Nutrien's leaders ensured all sites were supplied with both information and equipment to correctly set up to protect staff and enable them to work safely among themselves and their customers. From a big picture perspective, Nutrien's role in continuing to feed Australians was self-evident.

Nutrien's manufacturing sites were quickly re-tooled to make hand sanitiser, which was distributed not only to Nutrien stores but also to their clients, competitors, and critical community services such as police stations, at no charge. As an industry leader, Rob understood that all industry participants needed to continue to operate for the country's sake. When competitors called to ask what Nutrien was doing, Rob and his fellow leaders shared the documents and messages they had sent to staff and customers. The start of the pandemic was not a time for petty tribalism.

At the other end of the scale, a self-employed electrician sub-contracts to a company that services shopping centres in New South Wales and Victoria. They replace light globes for tenants within the shopping centre. Typically, the electrician receives 50% of the value of the work he does for himself. If a job is worth $1,000, he earns $500.

Due to restrictions caused by the government's lockdown laws, shopping centres effectively became ghost-towns overnight, and tenants closed their doors. Work for the electrician dried up. Other than the odd job, little work was available. The business owner contacted the electrician and informed him that, during the pandemic, his invoices were to represent 85% of the fee. In other words, if a job was worth $1,000, the electrician was to invoice $850.

The electrician did not ask for this support. Instead, the owner was proactive in providing it to him. How do you think the electrician feels about this support?

If you said he feels fantastic, you would be correct.

Norman Same and his fellow partners at accounting firm KNP Solutions in Melbourne, Australia, predicted a lockdown would occur a week before the Australian government announced the first lockdown. Incredibly, KNP Solutions conducted a trial of all staff working from home. Each team member took their computer, keyboard, and mouse home. The company had already delivered two screens to each person's residence. As a result of the trial, they identified a series of challenges that would require resolving before any official lockdowns occurred. Upon returning to the office, one staff member left their mouse at home. Norman and his partners quickly realised that all equipment needed to be duplicated at home to ensure staff could easily switch from the office to home without worrying about taking equipment with them. It was going to be hard enough being isolated from each other. Still, they didn't want the staff to have to worry about equipment. Their systems were already cloud-based, so the switch was possible, but without the trial, they wouldn't have discovered that the internet service at some of their staff member's homes was inadequate and would not support working on the cloud. Norman and his partners solved this challenge by providing powerful dongles to those staff members.

When meeting via Zoom, after initial introductions where everyone could see each other, they agreed to turn off their videos to help staff using dongles cope with the volume of bytes moving up and downstream. While not all dongles had been received by the start of the first lockdown, the fact that Norman and his fellow leaders were proactive with their trial meant they were ahead of the game. The dongles arrived within weeks of the first lockdown, which would have been months later (and caused significant disruption to KNP's ability to serve their clients) if KNP Solutions had not been proactive in identifying this problem as quickly as they did.

When the government released the Job-Keeper and Job-Seeker support packages, KNP Solutions offered their clients six weeks of complimentary support. They used this time to help their clients understand what the packages meant for their businesses. If they had not been set up as they were, providing this type of support for their clients would have been nearly impossible.

When leaders control what they can control, demonstrate foresight, and show genuine care for the people in their organisation, it is no surprise that staff respond in kind. Throughout the pandemic, productivity has increased at KNP Solutions which is a credit to the entire team.

Shortly after the commencement of the first lockdown in April 2020, Andrew Buxton, managing director of MAB Corporation in Melbourne, Australia, called a staff meeting. He reassured all staff that the company's main priority was ensuring that everyone's job was safe. While some working from home had been occurring, it certainly hadn't involved all staff. Computers, tables, and chairs were ordered and supplied to facilitate all team members having the appropriate equipment to work from home. All leaders were informed to do what was necessary to support staff throughout the transition to working from home.

David Allt-Graham, general manager, Residential, knew that one of his team members was in a challenging situation. Mike Stasiuk's wife and youngest son were in Norway with her family, and the airlines had cancelled their return flights due to the global lockdowns that occurred at the start of the pandemic. Mike also had his eldest son with him, who had just commenced his primary school education. Like many parents, Mike would have to home-school his son, work from home, and maintain contact with his wife and son in Norway. David quickly realised that it might be quite some time before Mike would know when his wife and youngest son would be able to return to Australia. With his own young family, David empathised with Mike's situation.

David reassured Mike that he had complete control over his time. He was encouraged to focus on home-schooling his son as required, and if he needed time in the afternoon to connect with his wife and son in Norway, he was given support to do so. David understood that it would take Mike a few weeks to work out a schedule that would work for him and his circumstance. Mike is a high performer by any definition. With the freedom and autonomy provided by David and MAB, he continued to perform at a high level while home-schooling his eldest son throughout more than 180 days of home-schooling during 2020. In addition, it wasn't until 26th December 2020 that his wife and youngest son were reunited with him in Australia.

Mike's story is an example of the genuine human reality that millions of people have faced and continue to face due to the pandemic. MAB Corporation was not responsible for Mike's situation. But their support and genuine care for him enabled him to get through an unbelievably difficult time while he continued to deliver value for the organisation. At the time of writing, more than 20 months after the initial lockdown, no one at MAB Corporation has lost their job due to the pandemic. Andrew Buxton has been faithful to his word.

Notice the pattern in these positive examples. The leaders were all **proactive** in their actions. Proactivity is the first habit in Stephen Covey's seminal book, *The 7 Habits of Highly Effective People*. As a leadership behaviour, proactivity works. But first, you must assess what you believe about leadership.

Chapter Two
Start by assessing your mental models

How do you know if you are a 21st century leader? First, you must assess your core beliefs about leadership. What do you believe are the characteristics of an effective leader? What are the factors that you think will hold you in good stead? What are the three most important behaviours that you believe a leader must possess to be effective? If you are struggling to identify these behaviours, identify someone you know who you think is an example of a good leader. What are their leadership characteristics?

1. ____
2. ____
3. ____

The behaviours you have identified depend upon your mental models. A mental model is a theory about how the world works. They are formed throughout your life and are a culmination of your various life experiences. These include, but are not limited to:

- Your family situation
- Your education
- Your national culture
- Your language
- Your religion (or no religion)
- Your work experiences
- Your exposure to different cultures

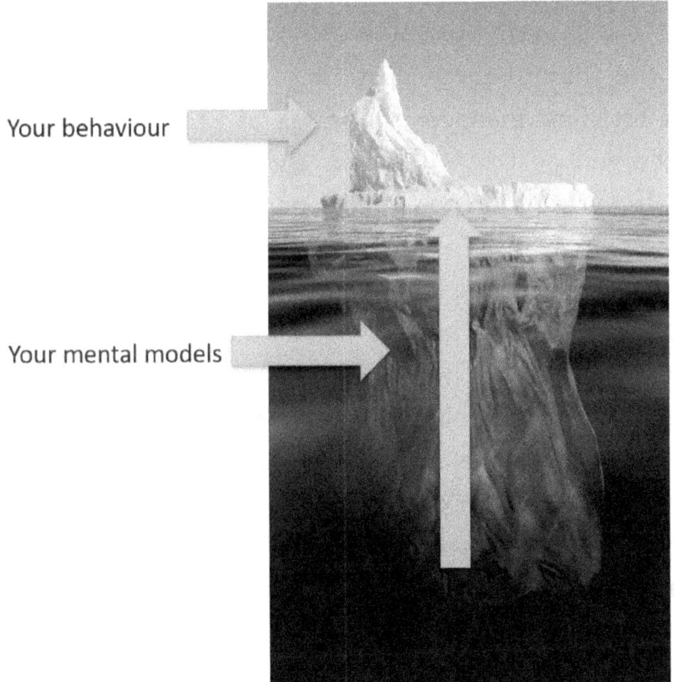

Figure 1: *The Iceberg Model*

Mental models are enormously powerful. They cause people to behave in ways that can appear irrational. Mental models are often "layered," which means one mental model influences another.

Consider an iceberg. Above the waterline is your observable behaviour. Below the waterline is your mental models. These are your theories about how the world works, some of which you will share with other people; in other words, you will share the same views. The challenge is that you are highly likely to be unaware of your theories until you learn about a concept such as mental models. You see, your mental models are not explicit. Yet, they have a direct influence on your behaviour. What if your mental models are flawed? But you aren't aware they are faulty, so you keep using them? Let me illustrate.

As a first-time manager at the age of 24, I led a team of eight staff, the youngest of whom was eight years older than me. All the staff were either part-timers or casual staff. I was the only full-time employee.

I was earning the big money of $23,400 per year. I had the title "Manager." I *thought* I had to have all the answers. When a team member came to me with a question, and I did not know the answer, what do you think was my most probable behaviour?

"Fake it until you make it!" I hear you say. That is precisely what I tried to do. I tried to "pretend" that I knew the answers instead of engaging with the team and working with them to discover the best solution. I did not tap into the experience and knowledge of the group. Sometimes, I would avoid the question and use my positional power to deflect the conversation to another topic.

Fortunately, this behaviour was observed by the organisation's general manager, who explained to me what mental models were and how I was behaving because of my subconscious theories. My general manager explained that mental models were not right or wrong; instead, it was their usefulness that mattered. Were my mental models influencing me to behave in a manner aligned with the type of leader I wanted to become, or were they influencing me to behave inconsistently? To answer this question, I had to become aware of my mental models.

Through reflection and reading, I discovered that it was likely I was behaving in this way because of a combination of several mental models, including:

- I am the manager, earning the most money of anyone in the team, so I need to demonstrate that I am worth that money and am therefore worthy of my salary
- Managers are the most intelligent people in their team; otherwise, they wouldn't be the manager
- Competent managers know a lot about a lot; therefore, I need to demonstrate how much I know, at all times if I am to be identified as being a competent manager

I had no idea why I had these mental models. My general manager suggested I read a book by Peter Senge, *The Fifth Discipline - The Art & Practice of The Learning Organization,* and start with the chapter on mental models. He then suggested, *"What if you adopt the mental model that you are a learner. Someone who is open to learning and will work with the team you lead and learn together, over time, and make this work better and better?"*

Without question, the single most influential lesson in my life has been the understanding that the more I am aware of my mental models, the more effective I can be as a person across all my life's roles. Mental models are so powerful they will overrule your values. Even though I believed in integrity, when my mental models about what I thought a leader ought to be were challenged,

I acted consistently with my mental models, not my value of integrity. As a leader, raising your awareness of your mental models is essential if you wish to be effective throughout the pandemic and beyond.

One of my favourite leadership books is Nelson Mandela's autobiography, *Long Walk to Freedom*. Nelson doesn't reference management theory, and he certainly doesn't talk about mental models. But he does describe significant changes in his thinking and mindset. In simple terms, Nelson shifted from believing that violence was the only way to rid South Africa of apartheid to practising peaceful resistance. His story is full of reflection and deliberate changes to his thinking that impacted his behaviour. One example includes a story that occurred after his release from prison, and he had become President of South Africa. While in a restaurant, Nelson invited one of his previous captors to share a seat at his table. The man was trembling. When one of his soldiers asked President Mandela why he would do such a thing when this specific goaler used to urinate on him after beating him up, Nelson replied, "The mentality of reprisals destroys states, while the mentality of tolerance builds nations."

Nelson Mandela could be excused for treating his captors with disdain. His biases toward them would be understandable. Yet, he made conscious decisions to keep his biases at arm's length and do what was necessary for his entire country, including his previous captors. Nelson was aware of his mental models and how they influenced his behaviour. When he discovered a mental model that was no longer useful, he adopted a new mental model and changed his behaviour. This lesson is extraordinary. It is not easy to change your thinking, yet if you want to be effective as a leader, you must be open to changing your mental models and resultant behaviour if you desire to be the best leader you can be.

Unconscious bias, diversity, and inclusion

In his book, *The Excellence Dividend - Principles for Prospering in Turbulent Times* from a *Lifetime in Pursuit of Excellence*, Tom Peters highlights that most boards and executive teams in corporate America do not reflect their customers' diversity. He asks a simple question, "Why not?" Suppose company boards and leadership teams do not reflect the diversity of their customers and the people they serve. In that case, they will not even be aware of the collective biases that influence their decision-making.

The challenge with our biases is that most are unconscious. Recognising that you have them is the first step, then having the courage to do something about them is the second. One of Australia's most successful boutique culture and leadership firms, Leading Teams, identified a challenge recruiting women. Only 7% of job applicants were women. How would they increase the number of female staff in the organisation if only 7% of respondents were women? What was stopping women from applying? One of Leading Teams' facilitators, Shelly McElroy, led a process where they discovered some research from Harvard University that highlighted that men would apply for jobs if they met 60% of the criteria. In comparison, women would apply if they met 100% of the requirements. Here was a clue.

Another clue was employee benefits such as flexible working rosters, parental leave, bonus structure, travel allowance, and car allowances were essential to women. Despite offering these benefits, they were not being included in their advertisements. They also ran a scan over the language used in their advertisements.

It was 92% male dominant. After just a single round of job advertisements where they corrected their language and included all essential benefits, their female application rate soared to 47%.

No one at Leading Teams had deliberately structured their advertisements to reduce the probability of women applying. Instead, the team at Leading Teams dared to challenge themselves to identify what they were doing that contributed to the problem. When they discovered the answers, they immediately addressed them and achieved an outstanding turnaround in just a single round of advertisements. What is your response to that challenge if you are in an organisation or industry with little diversity? Is it as simple as people from the underrepresented groups don't want to do that job? Or is there more to the challenge? What is in your control that you have not yet considered? Shelly and her colleagues dared to challenge themselves to be true to their purpose and remain open to opportunities to improve. With focus, attention, a willingness to be honest and to challenge themselves, Leading Teams discovered a solution that provided immediate benefits to the organisation.

Nutrien Ag Solutions Australia (Nutrien) is Australia's leading agricultural retailer employing more than 4,100 people in 700 locations throughout the country. Managing Director Rob Clayton recently celebrated the commencement of the second Women In Leadership program in June 2021. The first program was launched in 2020 because, as a male-dominated industry, Nutrien's leaders recognised they needed to take deliberate action to improve the ratio of women in senior leadership roles. The organisation formed the Nutrien Diversity & Inclusion Gender Working Committee, including Rebecca Staines, national seed category manager, whom I was coaching at the time, to

identify a range of initiatives to develop female leaders throughout the organisation. Despite the pandemic having commenced,
Rebecca and her colleagues set targets and initiated programs.

The committee's target, approved by Nutrien's Executive, was
to have 18% women in leadership positions before the end of
2021, which has already been achieved. A longer-term target is
to have a minimum of 32% women in leadership positions by the
end of 2026. These might look like they are just numbers, but that
is not accurate. A significant amount of work to attract women
into the industry and identify and provide networks and path-
ways for them to develop their leadership skills, if that is what
they choose to do, is available for them. The Women in Nutrien
Mentoring program has matched emerging leaders with mentors
both inside and external to the organisation. A surprising benefit
of the pandemic and pivoting to online-only activities increased
the program's reach beyond Australian shores, enabling the 23
women in the two Women In Leadership cohorts to work with
successful men and women within the industry.

Kristina Hermanson is the managing director of FMC Australia
– New Zealand (FMC ANZ), a subsidiary of FMC Global. FMC
is an agricultural sciences company that has 95 employees in
Australia and five employees in New Zealand. Kristina is passionate about enabling more women to have the opportunity to
develop into senior leadership roles within the agricultural industry. Despite the pandemic, in 2021, FMC launched the FMC LEAD
Scholarships Program. Aspiring women aged 18 to 35 from across
the agricultural sector in Australia and New Zealand were able to
apply for two scholarships valued at more than AUS$12,000 to
enable them to progress toward senior levels of leadership. When
announcing the inaugural awardees on 8th July 2021, Kristina said,

"Seeing more young female graduates entering the sector is promising, but the key is bringing that diversity through the ranks to senior management to continue building diversity in decisions and strategic direction." A unique aspect of the program is that anyone who entered the program will continue to participate in a series of ongoing networking events. Initially, these events will be online but will move to in-person as soon as possible.

Leading Teams, Nutrien, and FMC ANZ have continued their essential journeys on this topic throughout the pandemic. They didn't stop because other things were more important. They have continued with their efforts because this type of work is fundamental to future success. The disruption caused by the pandemic has forced organisations to identify and focus on the essential issues. Like many others, the fact that Leading Teams, Nutrien and FMC ANZ have continued to focus on enabling more women to enter their industries and support them to advance their careers indicates they are serious about this issue and are taking deliberate action to improve.

Diversity and inclusion are not just about gender. The Diversity Council of Australia defines diversity and inclusion as:

> **Diversity** *refers to the mix of people in an organisation – that is, all the differences between people in how they identify in relation to their:*

- *SOCIAL IDENTITY e.g., Aboriginal and/or Torres Strait Islander background, age, caring responsibilities, cultural background, disability status, gender, religious affiliation, sexual orientation, gender identity, intersex status, and socio-economic background.*

- *PROFESSIONAL IDENTITY e.g., profession, education, work experiences, organisational level, functional area, division/ department, and location.*

These aspects come together in a unique way for each individual and shape the way they view and perceive their world and workplace – as well as how others view and treat them.

Inclusion *refers to getting the mix of people in an organisation to work together to improve performance and well-being. Inclusion in a workplace is achieved when a diversity of people (e.g., ages, cultural backgrounds, genders, perspectives) feel that they are:*

- *RESPECTED for who they are and able to be themselves;*
- *CONNECTED to their colleagues and feel they belong;*
- *CONTRIBUTING their perspectives and talents to the workplace; and*
- *PROGRESSING in their career at work (i.e. have equal access to opportunities and resources).*

It is only through inclusion that organisations can make the most out of diversity.
(https://www.dca.org.au/di-planning/getting-started-di/ diversity-inclusion-explained)

Recognising and acting on these issues is essential for organisational success. Research from Deloitte indicates that diverse teams produce 2.3 times higher cash flow than non-diverse teams. Improving diversity is great for human beings, great for leaders and great for business. Why wouldn't you do it?

The knowing-doing gap

Leaders often believe they know how to execute their skills. For example, the leaders I usually coach think they're good listeners. They think they know how to listen and believe their behaviour matches their view of themselves. Yet, when I observe them interacting with their colleagues, they talk over the top of them, ask poor quality questions and don't execute the listening skills they believe they possess.

This is the Knowing-Doing Gap. In their seminal book, *The Knowing-Doing Gap*, Pfeffer and Sutton wrote about how smart companies turn knowledge into action. You believe you both know how to execute a skill and are competent when you do it. However, when your behaviour is observed, a gap exists. You are not behaving as you believe.

Of course, I am fortunate to work with many excellent listeners. They are concerned about maintaining the quality of their listening and wish to focus on keeping the gap as small as possible. It is always one of the main goals of the work we do together. They understand that if they take their eye off this skill, even for a moment, their competence will quickly recede.

Frank Catalano, principal at Glen Waverley Primary School in Melbourne, Australia, is one example. When Frank commenced as principal in July 2010, the school had 320 students and ranked within the 60th percentile for performance for the state's 1,600 public primary schools. Today, the school has 911 students and has maintained its rank in the 95th percentile for performance since 2014. The school is one of only eight schools throughout Australia to have achieved and maintained registration to the Council of International Schools (CIS) membership standards. Without question, Frank and the 85 staff he leads are high-performers.

The pandemic has tested every element of their high-performance mindset. Throughout the past 20 months, the school has switched from on-site to remote learning more times than anyone can count. Each time the school has pivoted to learning from home, Frank and the school leadership team have challenged themselves to remain consistent with the school's core philosophy, which is:

- The students are at the centre of everything we do
- Building staff capacity is paramount
- Everything we do is based on research and a whole school approach

Frank has consistently challenged his leaders to use the pandemic as an opportunity to reassess how the school does what it does to remain consistent with its philosophy. There is no point in having a philosophy if all it does is sit on the walls of the school buildings. In January 2020, the school had 80 students who required special needs. This was just under one-tenth of the student population. That number has swelled to more than 350 students throughout 2021. Using the lens that the school philosophy provides, Frank and the leadership team have worked with their colleagues to identify students who need extra support from a well-being perspective – listening to students, parents, and each other has been the cornerstone behind creating more support for students.

One of the school's popular bi-annual events is its production. Usually, the production results in the whole school community working and creating a special event. That cannot happen in 2021. The current laws won't allow the school community to gather as they did in 2019. Instead, each class prepares their video-taped performance when on-site learning is possible, and the main cast records their parts. The school's media team will create a video version of the production. An evening will be scheduled where the show will be streamed into the school community's homes for everyone to witness the final product together, as if they were together, in person. Relevant teachers have been provided time away from their standard classes to prepare for the event. Once again, Frank, the leadership team, and staff were guided by their school philosophy to "find a way" to enable the bi-annual production to occur, despite the constant uncertainty associated with lockdowns and the return to remote learning.

A school philosophy exists for a reason. It exists to inform action, which can take time to build into your culture. Frank and the team at Glen Waverley Primary School have become masters at closing the Knowing-Doing-Gap. If your organisation has a set of principles or a philosophy intended to guide and inform your actions, how big is your gap? What is your evidence?

Push through the learning curve

In Seth Godin's book, *The Dip*, he explains that the world doesn't progress in straight lines. Instead, the world moves in curves and circles. Learning is the same. When you start to learn something new, typically, you experience a slight improvement at the start. Then you become stuck. Either you persist at this point with what you are learning, or you quit. Throughout my experience, I have learned that professional people have an inflated perception of their ability to learn something new. Not all people have this increased perception, but it is more common than not.

When asked to rate themselves out of ten for the statement, "When I learn something new, I master it very quickly," most respondents in my workshops have scored themselves seven or more out of ten.

The rating does not match how many of you learn. Instead, you start at three or four out of ten. Initially, you are further from mastering the new technique than you like to admit. As a professional, your mental model is that you are a quick learner. It is what separates you from everyone else. It is a crucial differentiating factor. To admit that you must put extra effort to learn something new, such as a conversation technique, is paramount to realising that you aren't as competent as you like people to believe.

Instead of putting in the extra work, you blame the technique. "It doesn't work," you exclaim. Then, you find something new and repeat the process. Eventually, you risk developing an anti-learning mental model. "All those techniques are just theory, and they don't work in the real world!" Hmm, isn't that statement itself representative of a theory?

Exponential curves all work the same. At the start, there is a slight performance improvement, even though time is progressing. The curve is relatively flat. The initial effort is providing little to show for it. If you can recall learning to ride a bicycle or have taught someone to ride, you will quickly understand this concept. Attempt. Crash. Attempt. Crash. Attempt. A little success, then, crash! If the person you are teaching is a child, there is usually a few tears (learning doesn't always have to hurt, of course!). Eventually, the successes start to come. Suddenly, the riding technique kicks in, seemingly out of nowhere, and the child rides hundreds of metres without crashing. And, instead of crashing, they manage to put their feet down when they get the wobbles and stop themselves from crashing. Then, the wobbles start to disappear and off they go, able to ride with you. This process occurs over three days for most children I have trained.

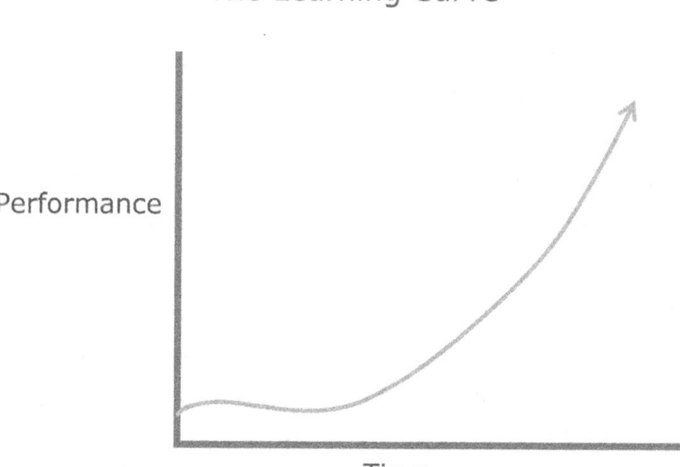

Figure 2: *The Learning Curve*

Learning nearly always follows this pattern. The beauty of an exponential curve is that you cannot reach the curved part without first progressing through the flat portion. When you recognise that a skill is something you want to learn because it will benefit your future, learning to "push through the curve" is essential.

Daniel Auld, director at Eric Jones Stairbuilding Group, did something unusual in his industry in the last quarter of 2019. With support from his HR manager, Sandra Marinacci-Orbach, he engaged my services to work with his frontline leaders within his timber staircase division. Unlike most people, Daniel and Sandra didn't want a single workshop that would magically improve their

leaders' skills over three hours. They believed they needed something more consistent, such as a program that would support the
development of their leaders over time.

A significant focus was improving verbal communication and
ensuring the leaders communicated a consistent message to
their colleagues. When the pandemic caused the first lockdown,
the business was in a category where it was allowed to continue
to operate. Daniel met with the leaders involved in the program,
Joe Van Roosmalen, Sam Kane, Matt D'Orazio and Stefano
Bianchi, to determine how they would protect themselves and
the business from the consequences of a COVID outbreak
on-site. They decided to create a split-shift system to prevent
the virus's possible spread and reduce the risk of shutting down
the entire operation. These conversations were not easy, and
the leaders had to engage with the members of their teams to
ensure their views were considered. Commencing an evening
shift required at least one of the leaders be present, and Sam
volunteered, offering himself because he felt that the impact on
himself and his family was less than it would have been for his
colleagues.

As soon as restrictions allowed, Daniel and Sandra were eager
for the program to continue. So, too, were Joe, Matt, Stefano,
and Sam. They knew they had learned a lot, but there was more
to learn. They wanted to continue to push through the learning
curve.

Following COVID-safe protocols, we met outdoors in the carpark. We maintained physical distancing, and I used a mobile
whiteboard to share the agenda and workshop challenges as they
arose. At the end of the first session outdoors, Stefano shared
that he was having a challenge maintaining the performance of

the members of his team who were working the evening shift. While he did a hand-over with Sam every day, he wasn't there during the shift, so they were "without a leader." We then had a terrific conversation. Sam was present for the evening shift, but it hadn't been formalised with all the staff working the shift that he was their formal leader for as long as they would require the shift. As soon as it was no longer required, the team members would return to reporting to Stefano.

The leaders agreed this vital information would be communicated with the evening shift team members. Soon after this session, Stefano reported the performance of the evening shift returned to the expected level. A single question from him led to a conversation that produced a solution that positively impacted performance.

As COVID restrictions allowed, we continued the program in the carpark. During this period, the company moved to new premises. Moving location can be a challenging experience for any company but completing it during a pandemic added another layer of complexity. The leaders' communication skills were tested repeatedly. Various delays outside the team's control resulted in the move finally being completed three months later than first planned. In addition, numerous lockdowns came and went, constantly challenging the smooth operation of the organisation. Never had the communication skills of the leaders been as regularly tested. However, by maintaining the program, each leader focused on the skills they had been taught and continued to utilise them daily. Re-work has reduced, and the quality the team proudly delivers has been maintained throughout multiple lockdowns and a change of premises — what an outstanding achievement!

Words matter

Words have meaning. When you speak with other people, you use words to convey your intended meaning. However, many leaders are not as conscious of the meaning of their words when they speak. Let us consider the question, *"Do you mind if I talk to you about an issue that arose late yesterday?"* On the surface, this sounds and looks fine. A single word can have a massive difference in the **meaning** conveyed in the sentence. As an example, imagine if the question was, *"Do you mind if I talk with you about an issue that arose late yesterday?"*

Did you spot the difference between the two questions?

If you are talking *"to"* someone, and that is what you think you are doing, what is the likelihood of you listening to what they have to say?

When you speak *"with"* someone, it conveys the intent of being equal contributors to the conversation. Try it. Notice the difference this **one** word makes to how you behave in a conversation, assuming you do want to speak "with" them and not "to" them!

You may think these are just words, and does it matter? I have witnessed leaders talk "to" people throughout my coaching, and leaders speak "with" people. When they talk "to" people, everyone knows the positional power of the leader. Listening is expected to occur, but those spoken "to" are expected to do the listening. **Not the leader**.

I have had the enormous honour of facilitating leadership workshops with leaders from the Kingdom of Saudi Arabia, Japan, China, Indonesia, and throughout Australia. Listening has consistently been identified as a critical characteristic of effective leadership irrespective of the group I have worked with. Listening is an essential practice if you want to be an effective leader, no matter your religion, culture, or country of birth.

Words do matter. They have a meaning which is transferred to your behaviour. If you say that listening is essential, but you talk "to" people, what you "say" and what you "do" will not be aligned. Do you think people can spot the difference between what a leader "says" and what they "do"? Yes, of course, they can. What impact do you think this has on trust? Does it increase or decrease trust? The most likely outcome is trusting will go down. Maybe by only one marble, but it will still go down.

Consider, for a moment, the terms *human resources, human capital,* and *human assets.* What are the mental models that underpin these words? Are human beings resources? Are they capital? Are they assets? Resources, capital, and assets can be bought and sold. Are we saying humans can be bought and sold? Isn't that slavery, and isn't it against the law? Why have we allowed the meaning of these words to permeate so profoundly throughout organisations?

Part of the reason is that people do not spend much time thinking about the meaning of the words they are using. Just because you might not think too deeply about the words you choose to use does not change the meaning of those words.

Consider the phrase, "My team." Leaders use this phrase all the time. It implies that you own your team. Do you own the people you lead? Of course, you do not, but this phrase is used again, again, and again. What behaviours could result from the mental model that you "own" your team? As a leader, ought you not be considered with the words you use so they reflect the meaning you intend? "This is the team I lead" may better represent reality.

Equally, leaders ought to be "learners." In her book, *Mindset – How You Can Fulfil Your Potential*, Carol S. Dweck explained the science behind a *growth* mindset versus a *fixed* mindset. Her work resonated and made sense to me. A growth mindset means that you are open to learning. Garry Ridge and the tribe at WD40 have deliberately shifted from using the term *"mistakes"* to *"learning moments."* Tribe members learn to own their roles and to take responsibility for them. Unplanned and unexpected events do happen. Those involved take responsibility for the event, identify what can be learned, and assess if the learning will help WD40 improve for both the tribe members and their customers. If the lesson benefits both tribe members and customers, they implement it.

This mental model is encouraged at all levels of the organisation. It is okay for senior leaders to have "learning moments," too. A growth mindset has been deliberately established in the culture at WD40, and learning is expected to occur at all levels of the organisation (which is not as simple as it sounds). A growth mindset is characterised by the statement, *"I haven't learned this yet!"* The word "Yet" is critical. It implies that you will have done what you needed to do to learn whatever you need to know in the future.

A fixed mindset focuses on proving and establishing how great you are based on past performance, driven by your innate abilities. The fixed mindset believes that ability is what it is and cannot be developed over time. Incremental learning is okay because it is built on what you already know. However, suppose learning exposes the learner to something they believe they *should* have previously known. In that case, the fixed mindset will cause the leader to avoid the learning opportunity because admitting they need to learn something is akin to admitting they are incompetent. This situation is a phenomenon I call the **leader-learner trap**.

The leader-learner trap

Successful people regularly report they are lifelong learners. They espouse that they have a growth mindset.

Shayne Elliott, CEO of the ANZ Bank in Australia, shared a LinkedIn video post that he is *"#always learning."* In it, he speaks about a book that has provided tremendous value over many years, *Execution – The Discipline of Getting Things Done* by Larry Bossidy and Ram Charan. It is a terrific book and worth the read.

The ability to learn is essential for success. However, **are followers tolerant of leaders who are learning?** I am not sure they are, which creates a significant problem for leaders.

For example, if something goes wrong at the ANZ Bank and Shayne turns to his shareholders, stakeholders, board, and staff and says, *"Look, I don't know what to do in this situation. I'm a fast learner, and with the amazing people in the team, I'm confident we can work out a solution as soon as possible,"* do you think his stakeholders will be happy?

The odds are firmly stacked in favour of Shayne's stakeholders **NOT** being happy. They would expect that he should already know what to do for the pay he has been receiving.

This problem exists at all levels of leadership. And the more senior you become, the more significant this problem becomes. Followers expect that their leaders, because of their title, position, experience, and most of all, pay, should already know what to do when things go wrong. They believe that leaders should have previously known what to do first so that whatever went wrong would have never gone amiss in the first place.

The tolerance for leaders to be *#alwayslearning* is extremely low.

This pressure affects leaders in many ways. The most common effect is that leaders subconsciously associate their need for learning to signify they are incompetent. I have never met a single person who wants to be known for being incompetent. The thought of being perceived as incompetent catalyses fear in most people. As Professor Amy Edmondson says, "Interpersonal fear reduces learning behaviour."

The easiest way for leaders to avoid being "incompetent" is to do the very opposite to what they ought to do. They do not share or admit they are learning. Instead, they blame others, seek scapegoats, get angry, persist with strategies that are not working and generally cause the situation to worsen.

An interesting phenomenon is that the more significant the learning opportunity due to the gravity of the error, the less likely learning is to occur. Ultimately, this is not great for the leader, their followers, or the organisation.

One thing to say is that leaders need to be more emotionally intelligent, authentic, and open about their learning. Still, it is an entirely different scenario when something goes wrong, and followers believe that the leader *"Should have known better."*

While most people agree that leaders ought to be lifelong learners, the actual practice of being a lifelong learner often results in followers perceiving that their leader is incompetent. In turn, this drives down learning behaviours and drives up defensive routines. First described by Harvard University Professor Chris Argyris many decades ago, these are behaviours driven by a subconscious need to be competent. It is a compelling need and will cause good people to behave poorly. Leaders become trapped; while they want to learn, **they cannot be seen to be learning** because that would be a public admission that they did not know what to do in the first place and were therefore incompetent.

Think about it? Are people tolerant of leaders not knowing how to do something in your organisation? What pressure was applied, implicitly or explicitly, to leaders to understand what to do when the pandemic first appeared? As more information has become available, and hindsight has shown that some political leaders' actions should have been different from what they were, are leaders chastised for not having had this hindsight before making their original decisions? As leaders have changed tactics because of new information, how have their constituents responded? Many have been frustrated and angry, accusing the leaders that they "should have known better."

These issues highlight the complexities that underpin real learning at the most senior levels. What can you do about the Leader-Learner Trap? In her book, *The Fearless Organization*, Professor Amy Edmondson from the Harvard Business School advocates that leaders must take responsibility for creating the psychological safety that supports learning at all levels of the organisation. In doing so, leaders will reduce anti-learning behaviours that manifest from the leader-learner trap. There is no quick fix, but here are three interdependent strategies to get you started:

1. Validate learning as an essential element of every person's role, including senior leaders. Have leaders regularly

share stories that highlight what they have learned during crisis-free times. When crises occur, the learning culture established by these stories will help minimise knee-jerk blaming and avoiding action that germinates from anti-learning behaviours.

2. Create opportunities for diagonal slices of the organisation's hierarchy to learn together and be explicit that one's title is left at the door when staff enter the learning room. When people learn together on essential organisational tasks, staff can see the value of learning for everyone, including senior leaders, and their learning tolerance increases.

3. Adopt the WD-40 philosophy established by CEO Garry Ridge: there are never mistakes, only "learning opportunities." This shared mental model requires a commitment to eliminate the word "mistake" from your organisation's vocabulary. Aaah, yes, I can hear you say, "What? Are you suggesting that it would be a mistake to say the word mistake?" No; I am suggesting it would be a learning moment!

Mental models to consider

Employees are human beings, not human resources

Dee Hock, CEO Emeritus, and founder of VISA International, was right. Employees are human beings. They are not human resources. Keep this front of mind when you are making decisions about people. Bob Chapman, CEO of the US$3 billion Barry-Wehmiller group of companies, with over 12,000 people in its employment, says that his main concern during the pandemic is showing that he cares for its employees. The best way to do that is to re-affirm they have a job, and the company will work with them to keep them employed. To achieve this, a company must have a business model that can sustain down-turns. Economies go up, and they go down. They always have, and they always will. Chapman says that companies ought to continually work on their business model to ensure that it can benefit from the economy going up but sustain periods when the economy goes down. Since 1990, Barry-Wehmiller had experienced eight downturns of various magnitudes. Not once, during any of those downturns, did the company stand down an employee. Bob says, *"Leadership is the stewardship of the lives entrusted to you, to bring out the best in the people we have the privilege of leading. Management is the manipulation of others for your success."* When you lead people, they do extraordinary things. When you manage them, they give you less. If you are a so-called hard-nosed business person, sustained financial success will be achieved by leading people instead of managing them. This mental model underpins all that follow.

Learning and oxygen are equally crucial for human beings

If you cease having access to oxygen, what will happen?

You will die. Equally, if you stop learning in an ever-changing world, what is the most likely impact that will have on your career? Metaphorically speaking, it, too, will die.

Continuous learning is essential for performance and career success. Garry Ridge, CEO of WD40, says that WD40 employees do not make mistakes. As you read earlier, the word "mistake" has been deliberately eliminated from their vocabulary. Instead, they have "learning moments." They have used language to reinforce the mental model that learning matters, not blaming someone when things do not work out as planned.

What are your mental models about learning? Do you take responsibility for it? Or do you consider your education to be the responsibility of someone or something external to you? Anders Ericcson, the author of *Peak – How All of Us Can Achieve Extraordinary Things* and the world expert on expertise, says that no one in the world has become an expert at anything without the willingness to do the hard work that comes with learning and mastering a subject. It turns out that hard work is the key, but a special kind of hard work makes the most significant difference.

Smart, hard work

According to Ericcson, no one achieves excellence without hard work. No-one. Period. And no one achieves excellence without doing *smart*, hard work.

Smart, hard work is discovering and mastering the most appropriate technique related to whatever you attempt to master. The opposite of smart, hard work is ineffective hard work. Ineffective hard work is when you do what you think you should be doing, but you practice the wrong thing because you have not done your research on what you should be doing. Ineffective hard work can feel like smart, hard work. Except, it is not. It is ineffective hard work. Let me illustrate the difference between smart, hard work and ineffective hard work.

When my daughter Sienna was in third grade, she joined her school aerobics squad. She was selected in the third level team. The first level team consisted of seven girls, all of whom were in fifth and sixth grade. The second level team included girls from the fourth, fifth and sixth grades. Sienna's team had girls from the third to the fifth grades.

While at different levels, each of the three teams competed against each other and all the other primary school teams. The first level team won the state championship, which automatically qualified them for the national championships. Both the second level team and Sienna's team failed to qualify for the national championships.

Later that year, the first level team won the national championship. This achievement meant that the school would be required to compete at a higher level the following year, even though all the girls in the national championship-winning team would no longer be at the school.

Three days into the start of the following school year, while our family was eating dinner, Sienna made a statement. *"I'd love to be in the first level team this year, but it's impossible!"*

"Why is it impossible?" I inquired.

"Well, you know that I was in the third level team last year. And we didn't qualify for the national championships. And, because we won the gold medal, we have gone up another level as a school. Plus, no girl has ever made the first-grade team without being in year five or six, and I'm only in fourth grade this year. Dad, it's impossible!"

"When are the trials?" I asked.

"About six weeks away," Sienna replied.

"Okay, let's imagine you **can** *make the first level team. What could you do between now and the trials to make that team?"*

"Hmm, I could train," Sienna said.

"How often?"

"Every day?" she said.

"For how long, each day?"

"Hmmm, ten minutes?"

"*Yes, that sounds fine!*" I said, smiling to myself.

"*Okay,*" I continued, "*You could train each day for ten minutes. Is there anything else you could do?*" I asked.

"*Umm, I could ask my friends to join me?*"

"*Yes, that sounds like a great plan. Anything else?*"

"*Hmmm, maybe I should ask my teachers what training we should be doing?*"

"*That's a brilliant idea! That way, you'll be doing the correct training, the sort of training that will help you have a chance at getting in the first level team,*" I replied, smiling broadly.

We concluded the conversation.

Importantly, when Sienna went to school the following day, she recruited two friends to train with her. She spoke with the teachers, who were passionate about aerobics, and asked about the sort of training they should be doing to give them a chance of making the first level team. Then, they started training at recess and lunchtime. The teachers, who were also their coaches, would join them at lunchtime and provide extra coaching.

This is smart, hard work. Sienna and her friends were practising the correct technique. They could have just as quickly **NOT** asked the teachers about what training they should be doing and have trained in a manner that matched what they "thought" they should be doing. Equally, given their training commenced six weeks before the trials, what do you think the girls in the second level team the previous year were doing at recess and lunchtime at this time?

Whatever it was that they were doing, it was **not** training. Typically, the girls would start preparing two to three weeks before the trials. Frankly, training for the aerobics squad was not yet on their radar.

Given Sienna and her two friends, all in fourth grade, were training an hour a day across recess and lunchtime, and they were receiving coaching from the coaches of the team, how much do you think they improved before the trials?

In this example, the answer was a considerable amount of improvement. So much so that all three girls were selected in the first level team! Of the seven girls in the group, three were in fourth grade, and the rest were in sixth grade. Some of the girls from the previous year, who were in the second-level team, missed selection in the first-grade squad.

The girls continued to train hard and went to the state championships. Please recall that they were now competing at a higher level of competition compared to the previous year. They won the state championship and automatically qualified for the national championships. This was an extraordinary effort, and the team went on and won the silver medal! The smart, hard work that Sienna and her two friends had done certainly paid off.

There are two essential elements for smart, hard work. The first element is that you are doing the correct work. This means that you have completed some research and found the "correct" work that you plan to master. When I say "research," I don't mean academic research, although, in some circumstances, that form of study may be appropriate. Usually, your research will involve finding an expert and obtaining the relevant information from them. For example, when Sienna sought advice from her coaches about what training she ought to do to prepare her for the trials, she completed the "smart" part of smart, hard work. The second element of smart, hard work is you put the time into practising and mastering the correct work, or as I like to call it, the Technique

That Matters. Practising the proper technique is the "hard work" part of smart, hard work.

Effective leaders help the members of the team focus on identifying and completing smart, hard work. The pandemic has provided leaders with an opportunity to clarify the essential tasks for each team member. Teaching team members to identify smart, hard work will have benefits well beyond the pandemic. And being clear about what is vital in your role is paramount for personal and organisational success.

Cash is king. Clarity is queen.

In the mid-1990s, I was introduced to the term "Cash is King." It means that, in business, you can never forget that accountants and finance rule the day. No matter where we live and work, we exist within an economic reality governed by the mighty dollar.

Everything that we do as leaders, ultimately, will be judged by its economic impact. Yet, I preach Servant Leadership, which is about recognising the full potential of people and enabling them to shine.

How does Servant Leadership align with the "Cash is King" concept?

Whether you like it or not, the number-crunchers rule the world. Period. Your organisation does not have to be "for profit" for this to be true. A not-for-profit government agency, and similar types of organisations also need to achieve their budget. No organisation is immune from this reality. The money that governments around the world have been pouring into their economies to keep them afloat (in Australia, Job-Keeper and Job-Seeker are two examples) is largely borrowed money that will have to be repaid.

I believe that the resourcefulness and capacity of human beings are primarily underutilised within organisations. This underutilisation of people costs companies a lot of money. It costs them the money they did not save because of poor decisions, and it costs them reduced productivity that results from people not working anywhere near their capacity.

Poor decisions and low productivity are both caused by a lack of clarity for employees, including:

- Clarity about roles.
- Clarity about what constitutes "doing a good job."
- Clarity about how their key responsibilities will be measured.
- Clarity about how their part fits with the functions of other members of the team.
- Clarity about how their role contributes to the broader organisation's purpose and why their role matters.
- Clarity about the relationships they need to nurture to perform their role effectively and achieve the results they are supposed to achieve.

When human beings are clear about what they must do, decision making becomes a lot easier, and productivity goes through the roof. Therefore "Clarity is Queen." Organisations need the king and queen working together to be successful.

Recently, the frontline leaders and business owner of an organisation I am working with made some changes to a process they had been doing for more than nine years. All the leaders "knew" the process was flawed and was creating re-work (the extra work that must be done to correct something that could have, and should have, been done the first time correctly). Why did they keep doing the process that they all (independently) believed was flawed? Because they were not clear that part of their role as leaders is to keep their eye out for flaws in their system and offer suggestions to correct those flaws. And, for that to occur, all of them, including the business owner, must be open to listening to each other's suggestions and not take these personally or as an assault on their competence.

Within four weeks of commencing their leadership program, this error had been corrected and would, throughout the year, cover the cost of the leadership program more than ten times over. And those performance improvements will continue year on year.

Let that sink in for a moment. As a direct result of improving their leadership, their organisation will be making significant year on year savings. From a logical perspective, will those savings increase the job security of the leaders and their team members? Of course, they will!

Servant Leadership is about developing the skills so that everyone is clear about what they must do. Servant Leadership drives "Clarity is Queen." The reality is, whenever there are "cash" problems, they are caused by a lack of clarity.

Whoever receives the output of your work so that they can do their work is a customer

As previously established, not everyone uses the term "customer." Whether you have clients, patients, students, or stakeholders, it is how you interact and engage with those "customers" which is what matters. It is the same for your colleagues.

When you choose to behave as if the recipient of your work is your customer, you will better serve their needs. If you are not sure what this looks like, think of your experiences as a customer. When you do not get what you expect, you feel frustrated. If you believe that you should have been communicated more effectively than you were, you get frustrated and disappointed. The same is true when you are a staff member.

As a leader, consider the tasks those team members you lead require you to do so they can do their job. Often, you will need to provide them with information to be clear about what they are doing. It may be as simple as providing them with the names of people you would like to attend a meeting they are arranging on your behalf. Maybe, it is clarity about the topics you want to be included in a report. When this information is not provided on time, delays are incurred, or staff submit incorrect work. This leads to re-work, which is a wasteful use of valuable staff talent and resources.

The same issue exists between staff, primarily when they work in different teams or departments. Teaching this mental model to staff within your team, department, or entire organisation will improve communication, improve efficiencies, and reduce wasteful work (and all the frustration that comes with it!).

Take responsibility and own your role, versus blame and excuses

When you have role clarity, it makes it easier to take responsibility for your job. When you do not have role clarity, it becomes easier to make excuses for your performance or blame others for what they did not do. In their book, *Extreme Ownership*, Navy SEALs Jocko Willink and Leif Babin are strong advocates for teaching team members to take full responsibility for their role, including when given tasks they do not understand. Rather than using a lack of understanding as an excuse for not doing something correctly, Jocko and Leif recommend that you ask questions to ensure you understand why something must be done when you truly own your role.

On their third tour in Iraq, Jocko and Leif were handed an order by their commanders. *"Do not leave the base for a mission without taking some Iraqi soldiers with you."* At the time, Iraqi soldiers were known as the worst combat soldiers in the world. When a firefight would start in front of them, they would turn, run, and indiscriminately fire their MK40s over their shoulders without looking at what they were shooting. Often, they would attack their own personnel. Jocko and Leif were perplexed. *"Are these idiot commanders trying to get us killed!"* They joined with their platoon members in denigrating their commanders. Although they were highly trained leaders, Jocko and Leif initially did not lead in this instance. Instead, they joined the pack and complained.

Then, Jocko and Leif asked themselves an important question. *"Do we understand **why** this command has been given? We think we understand, but do we **really** understand?"* And they asked, *"Do we believe that command is trying to get us killed? With all the money that had been invested in our training over the years, does it make sense that they would be doing their best to have Iraqi soldiers, not even the enemy, kill us?"*

Mid-level leaders often feel cornered by their senior leaders to undergo tasks that seem downright stupid. Rather than throwing your hands up and saying, *"Well, I don't understand!"* you would speak with whomever you needed to increase your understanding. So, Jocko and Leif did precisely that. They went to their commanders and explained that they did not understand the command. They needed to understand better why the order had been given. If they understood why the order had been delivered, then they could explain this reason to their team members, who, in turn, would be more likely to understand the command and then be in a better position to work out how to implement the order safely.

Jocko and Leif were told that, rightly or wrongly, their commanders had concluded that if the Iraqi soldiers did not start to learn how to look after their country themselves, then Jocko and Leif would be returning to Iraq with their teams time and time again. Their children and grandchildren (if they were in the armed forces) would also be returning to Iraq for generations to come. The USA had taken on the burden of protecting Iraq without building the capacity of the Iraqis to look after themselves. Today was to be the first day in correcting that error. A line had been drawn in the sand. If the USA was ever going to withdraw from Iraq, the Iraqis needed to learn how to defend themselves. Jocko and Leif's role was to work out, with their team, how they could safely take Iraqis on their missions with them.

While they did not like the order, Jocko and Leif understood why it had been given. When they communicated the reason for the order with their team members, they did not like it, but they understood it. With understanding, Jocko, Leif, and their team members were able to work out how to have the Iraqi soldiers safely join them on missions while also providing the Iraqis with invaluable learning opportunities. When human beings do not understand why they are meant to follow a course of action that does not make sense, it triggers chemicals that flood your body. The more leaders understand how the brain functions, the more they can effectively lead.

Chapter Three:
The triune brain

In the mid-1960s, American physician and neuroscientist, Paul D. MacLean, shared his theory, The Triune Brain. Simon Sinek referenced the model in his breakthrough book, *Start With Why*, where he describes how to use the model to inform how to explain or sell a concept to people in your organisation. More recently, Albert Rutherford published *Neuroscience and Critical Thinking*, providing a modern introduction to the theory. In its most straightforward format, The Triune Brain represents the evolution of our brain. If you were to view a vertical slice of your brain, you would notice that it is structured in three "layers." The first layer is the *basal ganglia*, which are found at the centre and base of our brain. Basal ganglia exist in every animal, including birds and reptiles. This part of the brain, our *reptilian brain*, developed early in evolution and is responsible for self-preservation behaviours such as feeding ourselves, the fight, flight, or freeze response and reproduction. Defending family and protecting property or territory are considered behaviours associated with this part of the brain. This part of your brain is focused on **now**. It does not consider the future or the past. It is focused on this moment.

Even in the modern era, our reptilian brain helps us detect danger before it happens and explains why you can "sense" when things are not quite right. In simple terms, this part of your brain likes the familiar but is wary and alert about the unfamiliar. The unfamiliar can produce both fear and excitement, both of which will cause your body to release adrenaline, a powerful chemical that prepares your body for action.

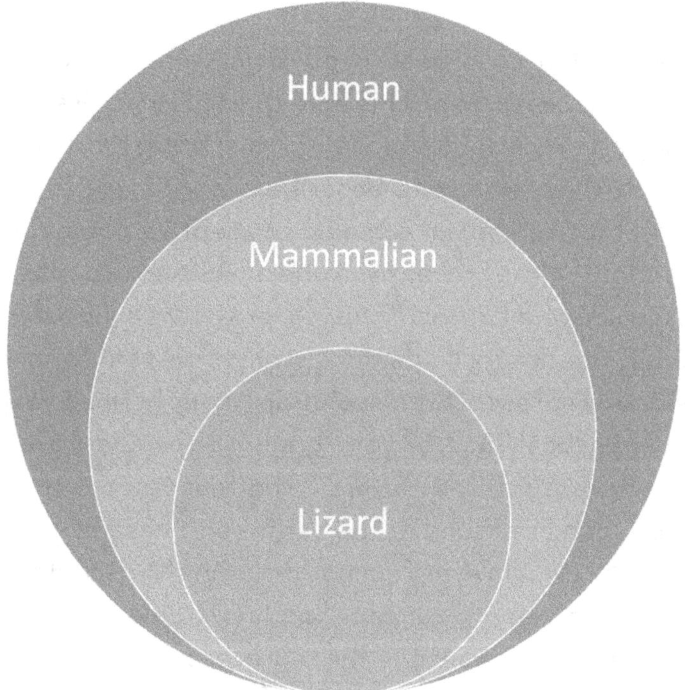

Figure 3: *The Triune Brain*

The second layer is the limbic system, which works closely with the basal ganglia. Our need for status, love and belonging comes from the interaction between the limbic system and the basal ganglia. MacLean argued that all mammals shared these needs, which is why he called it the Mammalian Brain. Consider a pride of lions. How do the members of the pride *know* who the lion king is? You may argue that he is the strongest and best fighter, which is true. But why do most lions seem to accept their "position" in the hierarchy? Only the rare lion challenges the leadership of the pride. When a young male lion loses a challenge against the lion king, what happens to it? It is expelled from the pride. The females, including their mother, usually support their expulsion. Unless it quickly joins with other expelled male lions, often its brothers or cousins, it will die.

Humans are no different. You need to belong. Everyone does. When you walk into a room of strangers, you cannot help but quickly assess "where you stand" within that group. It is an automatic response. When you detect where you stand, you will either agree with it and behave accordingly or reject it and equally behave accordingly (and risk being expelled by the group).

How do you think the mammalian brain coped with the isolation governments have implemented due to the COVID-19 pandemic? If you visited close family or friends during restrictions, you would have found it exceedingly difficult and quite odd not to have your usual physical contact with them, with hugs and kisses the standard form of communication. Your mammal brain will have desired this contact with people with whom you "belong." While walking down the street, it would have been relatively easy to maintain distance when walking past strangers. If a stranger did not try to help create some space between the two of you, you likely would have felt threatened, and your body would have been flooded with adrenaline. You may have even found yourself feeling angry. These two, quite different behavioural responses, are driven by these brain parts known as your emotional or irrational brain. Together, they make subconscious decisions and guide your emotions and "gut" instincts. Please note that the words "irrational" and "emotional" do not equal "wrong." Our reptilian and mammalian brains have served humans well over 200,000 years of evolution and have played a significant role in enabling our species to dominate the world. Throughout that period, our emotional brains have dominated our decisions.

The more aware you are of how these ancient parts of your brain affect your behaviour, the more you can take advantage of their strengths and limit their downside.

The neocortex forms the third layer of your brain. It is where the characteristics of being human stand out. This is where rational thought, logic, the ability to reflect on the past and imagine a future, and our capacity for complex language originate. It is known as the human layer.

The relationship between these three layers of your brain is essential to understand. The three layers are interconnected and interdependent, but the connection between the lizard and mammal brain to the neocortex is still evolving. Arguably, it is not as advanced as the connection between the lizard and mammal layers. In other words, the emotional and irrational layers of your brain play a significant role in your behaviour, and most of that role sits below the level of your consciousness.

As an experiment, imagine the last time you had a heated argument at work. As best you can, picture the person you were arguing with and what was said. "Feel" the debate.

Now, notice your body. What has changed? Has your heart rate increased? Do you feel warmer? If you felt annoyed during the argument, has that sense of annoyance returned?

All these reactions and changes to your state of mind and body result from chemicals flooding your body. These chemicals have been released due to you using your neocortex to recall a scene that your reptilian and mammalian layers of your brain have recognised as a fight, flight or freeze scenario, and they have prepared your body accordingly.

However, all you have been doing is sitting down. Because your mammal and reptilian brain live in the present, the memory generated by your neocortex stimulates the emotional part of your brain as if the event were occurring now. As a further experiment, recall a happy moment in your life. Notice the changes to your body. Now, remember a traumatic moment. Again, notice the changes to your body. Fascinating, isn't it?

As a leader, understanding how the brain works can assist you in being more effective with the people you lead. The pandemic has caused a disruption that has led to a high degree of uncertainty. Employees have been sent home and isolated from each other and, in some cases, from family and friends. No one knows when things will get back to "normal" or what "normal" even means. The "new normal" phrase has emerged to describe the new set of shared behaviours that will evolve from the pandemic. Which of the brain's three layers do you think remain on high alert?

The lizard and mammal layers of your brain, of course. As the emotional centre of our brain, it is little wonder the medical profession has been concerned about the adverse effects the pandemic is having on our mental health and well-being.

Mental health, wellbeing, and leadership

Graeme Cowan is a consultant, board director of R U O K, author of five books, and the *Caring CEO Podcast* creator.

He is passionate about assisting organisations in developing a caring culture that recognises stress in the workplace, which is often a significant cause of mental health challenges for employees.

In July 2021, Graeme interviewed Chris Murray, CEO of EnergyPower Systems Australia, an organisation with more than 240 employees based in ten branches across the country, including some with small staff numbers at the branch. The company has a turnover of approximately AUD $150M. In the interview, Chris shared his company's actions throughout the pandemic to show how leaders have cared for employees. Before February 2020, leaders regularly attended all sites to ensure they directly contacted each team member. Restrictions imposed because of the pandemic limited the movement of leaders and decreased this contact. At the time of writing, some new team members had not physically met their manager for more than 12 months. This lack of in-person communication is an example of the fundamental challenges of leading during a pandemic.

To counter this challenge, Chris and the senior management team increased their communication, including more Town Hall Calls (where all staff could attend the calls), online team sessions, and regular emails from the CEO. In addition, Chris engaged Graeme to train some team members to become *We Care Champions*. The role is not to act as counsellors but to be an additional point of contact for staff who, for one reason or another, do not feel comfortable sharing their challenges and stresses with their manager or members of the Human Resource team. All conversations with the *We Care Champions* are con- fidential and are conducted with empathy. Where appropriate, a range of actionable options are provided to the staff member who has sought support.

Please note that Chris has addressed the real issue that not all team members will share their problems, stresses, and challenges with their manager. In a perfect world, of course, team members would be comfortable having those types of conversations. But Chris recognises that we don't live in an ideal world. This reality is not a sign of poor leadership by the manager. Instead, it realises that there may be a myriad of reasons that a team member cannot speak with their manager that have nothing to do with the manager. But the conversations need to happen with someone if the problems are going to have any chance of being addressed and resolved.

Finally, Chris and his senior leadership encourage regular R U O K conversations between all staff, not just on RUOK day. I have included this example because it highlights, yet again, that there is no single silver bullet that demonstrates you see the people in your organisation as human beings. Instead, it is the accumulation of small actions, initiatives, and a constant desire to improve, understanding that on one level, you will never get to wherever "there" is! Performance matters, but so does caring for people. Chris emphasised this point when he expressed, *"If you don't care for your staff and make safety and wellbeing at the forefront of your business, then I don't think that will translate into good performance."*

Mindfulness matters

Associate Professor Craig Hassed and Dr Richard Chambers from Monash University, Australia, created a free online mindfulness course in 2015. The program continues to be available and has had more than 375,000 people worldwide enrol in the class to rave reviews. I participated in the second version of the course in February 2016.

The benefit of the course is that it provides practical tips for implementing mindfulness now, exactly when you need it. As a leader, you have a brain. You are human, too. The lizard and mammalian parts of your brain will be triggered, just like everyone else. You cannot stop the triggers and the flooding of chemicals around your body. But you can learn to recognise that you have been triggered and then do something about it. When the lizard and mammalian parts of your brain are activated, your sympathetic nervous system is stimulated, and your heart rate increases. The hairs on your arms rise. Blood is diverted to your large muscles. You ready yourself to fight, flight or freeze.

Managing your reaction to these triggers is essential for effective leadership. You don't want your behaviour hijacked by your emotional brain and cause unintended damage to your relationships with the people you lead. Three simple and effective techniques that Craig and Richard recommend are as follows:

1. Bring your attention to your feet. Notice the contact they make with the floor. If you need to, adjust the positioning of your feet so they are flat on the floor.
2. Bring your attention to your lower back and buttocks where it is in contact with your seat. Readjust your posture if you notice that you were slouching while maintaining your attention on the connection between your body and the chair.
3. Follow a breath in and out, six times in a row, without changing how you breathe. Simply bring it to your attention.

Each of these techniques triggers your parasympathetic nervous system. This system releases chemicals throughout your body that calm you. Your heart rate decreases, the hairs on your arms relax, your sweat glands stop firing.

Leading people requires you to understand how your brain works and leverage that understanding to ensure your behaviour supports rather than hinders the people you lead. Empathising with the people you lead, enabling them to connect with each other and the organisation, and enabling them to have as much role clarity as possible, will benefit all of you more than you can imagine.

Chapter Four:
Triple empathy, connection, and role clarity

Throughout the pandemic, the lizard and mammal parts of your brain are on high alert. It has been suggested that the brain is like Velcro to awful news and Teflon to good news. A heuristic is that the brain is attracted to bad news fourteen times more than it is attracted to good news. Why? While the good news is essential, bad news could kill you!

Megan Capicchiano, Culture Lead at one of Australia's leading universities, first used the term "Triple empathy, triple connection and triple clarity" in a conversation when we were preparing for several sessions I was conducting for the university. It beautifully articulated what I had been thinking and is a clear, simple, and practical set of strategies to assist with effective leadership during the disruption and beyond.

While each of the three strategies can be applied independently, their power comes from their interdependence. In other words, all three approaches are more powerful when used together, compared to only using one or two of them. Through implementing these strategies, a leader can lessen the probability that their behaviour and actions trigger the lizard and mammal layers of the brain of their team members in unhelpful ways. Instead, the leader's behaviour can calm and engage these parts of the brain positively.

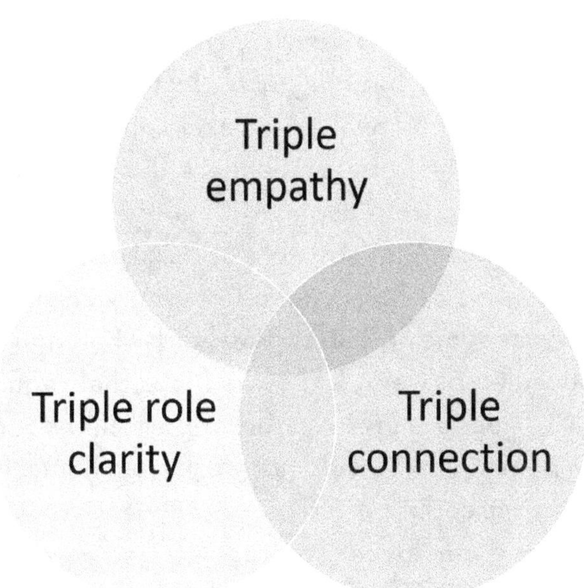

Figure 4: *Three Strategies To Calm The Brains of Employees*

Triple empathy

The global pandemic is both a shared experience and an individual one. While the news provides a constant reminder of the number of cases and deaths caused by the virus worldwide, which has created a shared understanding of the virus's impact, each person has their own unique experience of it.

A range of factors influences each person's experience of the pandemic. These factors include the number of people in their household, each of whom is also having their own unique experience of the pandemic; the circumstances of their dwelling and the amount of space it provides; access to quality internet and Wi-Fi (which in itself can significantly increase stress when it is inadequate); concern for relatives and friends, many of whom may live in countries where the virus has spread more rapidly; concern for partners and family members who may have an underlying condition that may increase their risk profile with the virus; and their personal, financial circumstances.

When the pandemic began, leaders did their best to find out how employees were coping with all the changes that had occurred. If some employees were at risk, i.e., they had under-lying health issues or family members who were a higher risk should they become infected, they did what they could to support those employees. If they had jobs that required them to be on-site, leaders investigated opportunities for them to work from home. If they could not work from home, they iden-tified leave that could be offered. Many leaders went above and beyond the employee "contract" to find ways to support them. Recall the CP Group offering food vouchers to families where a partner had lost their job in another company, sepa-rate to CP Group. As we move to a new phase of where you live alongside the virus, how will you continue to empathise with the people you lead? Consider employees living with a family member who has a severe and non-COVID-19 illness such as cancer. Despite being vaccinated, many immune-com-promised people remain at risk from COVID-19 and will con-tinue to be at risk while receiving treatment. As societies "open" and allow their populations to move more freely, the virus will continue to circulate, potentially increasing exposure to vulnerable people. How will you empathise and support these people?

Triple connection

As you have read, the mammalian brain needs connection. Are you sure that every person in your organisation receives regular, personal communication from leaders and team members? This is worth auditing. Ask the leaders who report to you to share how they connect with the people they lead and how the connection is cascading throughout the organisation. As leaders, ask yourself, "Are we leaving anyone out?"

Much of this connection does not have to be formal. A quick phone call, text message or instant message can be just as effective. Mixed with more traditional communication such as website updates, video messages, online meetings, electronic direct mail (EDM) and so forth, the informal connection is essential for the people in your team. Many organisations, such as Melbourne University Sport, set up a Friday afternoon quiz throughout the significant lockdown periods experienced throughout 2020 and again in 2021. Tim Lee, the Director of Melbourne University Sport, was delighted that several front-line team members catalysed the idea and followed through with help from their colleagues to make it happen. With support from senior leaders, the quiz commenced as a fun way for staff to connect and see who had the most knowledge on a wide range of hilarious topics. The host and theme of the quiz rotated between staff, and external contractors, such as me, were invited to participate. At the end of the year, 88% of staff involved in a coaching program independently named the quiz an essential and effective tool for maintaining a sense of belonging with the organisation and their teammates. Belonging, as you know, matters.

Leadership is not about being out the front and coming up with all the ideas and strategies for success. Instead, it is about enabling the people you lead at all levels of the organisation to believe they have both the responsibility and opportunity to make suggestions. They won't always come to fruition, but the possibility they may occur inspires staff at all levels to have the freedom to generate ideas and bring them to life when appropriate. Often, the ideas and actions do not have to be breathtaking and brand new concepts that no one else is doing. Instead, they can be simple and practical ideas and activities that work. That is precisely what happened at Melbourne University Sport.

How easy is it for staff at all levels to share ideas at your organisation? What is your evidence that staff regularly offer suggestions for improving how your organisation operates? How many of the concepts become a reality? How do you use those examples to generate similar behaviours from all staff?

Homewood Consulting is a small organisation with 18 staff who provide expert advice on managing trees in the landscape. As a provider of arboricultural services throughout Australia, Homewood Consulting has staff based in Victoria, the Australian Capital Territory and New South Wales. Ben Kenyon, director, and senior consulting arborist is a pragmatic person with strong family values. His pragmatism and values permeate through the business.

When the pandemic commenced, his first concern was ensuring the business survived so that the staff could have as much job security as possible. Border closures and city lockdowns immediately impacted the ability of his team to serve their clients. Typically, a staff team would fly to a location, for example,

Western Australia, and spend a week completing the data collection elements of their services and then return home to complete the required reports. Ben and his leadership team spoke with all staff to ensure that they understood that everyone would need to work together to get through this challenging period. If you have ever worked in a small business, you will know that staff don't sit around twiddling their thumbs. Under normal circumstances, there is always a lot of work to be done. At times, the various lockdowns and restrictions changed that reality for Homewood Consulting. Staff understood they needed to be agile and flexible. If there wasn't any work, they agreed they would use their leave balances to ensure they had an income. Meanwhile, Ben continued to work as hard as ever, finding new business.

In ambiguous times, such as those caused by disruption, the connection between team members becomes more important than ever. Reaching out and connecting with people, including activities and conversations that have nothing to do with work, matter more than ever. One of the simplest, yet profound changes Ben has initiated in his company, is the weekly staff meeting. Before the pandemic, these meetings would occur once every two months. Being connected and checking in has enabled everyone to understand that they are all in this together. They have solved many challenges. In late June 2021, Melbourne experienced severe storms that ravaged the entire state, particularly the Dandenong and Macedon Ranges. Trees required assessing immediately. As a result of the storm, some residential properties went without electricity for four weeks. Assessing trees so the clean-up operation could progress safely was paramount to opening roads and repairing power lines. Administration staff, who would usually not participate in operations in the field, volunteered to drive vehicles to increase the efficiency of the arborists evaluating trees. Although the 20-month-long pandemic continues and has created some difficulties for the business, Homewood Consulting is thriving, and productivity is higher than ever. When people are connected and have a common purpose, it is incredible what they can achieve.

Staff recognition aids in helping staff belong to your organisation and allows them to connect their work to the big picture. Raymond O'Flaherty, CEO of Metro Trains Melbourne, an organisation that employs more than 6,500 people from diverse backgrounds across Melbourne, immediately ensured that despite the pandemic dramatically reducing patronage, a key metric, his focus would be on supporting his colleagues. Between the commencement of the pandemic early in 2020 and mid-July 2021, Raymond posted 22 times on LinkedIn. On 19 of those occasions, Raymond recognised his colleagues, thanking them for their continued commitment to #OneTeamOneMetro and for facing the daily risk of performing their roles amid the pandemic. Instead of remaining in his office, Raymond's photos showed that he was onsite with his colleagues whenever possible. These messages were shared within the myriad of internal Metro Trains Melbourne communication platforms, ensuring staff knew their work mattered and was constantly recognised by the CEO. Several of the communications were unedited personal videos from his home, where Raymond reminded his colleagues of their critical role in keeping the city moving while keeping safety their number one priority in the conduct of their work. Using the term "colleagues" in his posts and videos highlights his commitment to the people he leads. Remember, words do matter!

Mario Stanisic, multi-modal authorised officers manager at Metro Trains Melbourne, leads 90 authorised officers. The team Mario leads ensure passenger safety and fare compliance across all modes of metropolitan and regional public transport services. At times, it can be a complex and challenging role. While passenger numbers have declined throughout the pandemic, the authorised officers have continued to perform their duties. They have been on the front line and have experienced the associated risks of working directly with the public during this period. The passengers they serve are understandably on edge. It is fair to say that most people want space around them, but that isn't always possible on public transport. Nor is the probability that all public transport users will follow the rules associated with mask-wearing, etc.

On Monday, 9 August 2021, the multi-modal authorised officers team celebrated 500 continuous days of zero Lost Time Injuries (LTIs). Would you please think about that statistic for a moment? Most of this period has been during the pandemic. Yet not a single authorised officer has had time off directly resulting from a workplace injury. When serving a public who is understandably on edge, the interpersonal skills required to achieve such an outcome are extraordinary.

Mario and his fellow leaders have deliberately focused on maintaining a connection with all authorised officers. Touching base and checking on how they are going and adjusting as required has ensured the team feel connected, and the essential role they have been performing for the city has remained at the forefront of their minds. The number of individual sessions, or sessions Mario has conducted with team members and their team leader, is too many to count. But they have happened and continue to occur. Why? Because connection matters! And when connection occurs, it is excellent for the team members, great for the leaders and fantastic for performance outcomes. Reducing LTIs is essential for staff because it means they remain healthy. It also reduces the costs associated with injuries which is great for an organisation's bottom line. When you lead well, it is good for both the people you lead and your bottom line. Both outcomes are 100% possible!

Being vulnerable enough to trust leaders at different levels of your organisation has proven essential for effectively connecting with staff. Michael Lewis, Stuart Major and Brett Cox are directors of ProctorMajor, an accounting firm based in the inner southeast of Melbourne, Australia. Initially, Michael, Stuart and Brett felt it was their responsibility to carry the lion's share of communicating and supporting the 23 staff in their business. In the process of recruiting two graduate accountants in August 2020, Michael, Stuart, and Brett were nervous about bringing in new team members who would be working remotely from their first day in the business. How would they support them, ensure they understood the culture and enable them to grow and develop from day one if they didn't receive in-person support? How could they be sure they would be efficient? These are great questions and understandable from the owners of a small business.

Senior accountants Hannah Jensen, Neil Walsh and Joy Gao let Michael, Stuart and Brett know they need not worry. Hannah, Neil, and Joy could support the new staff. *Leave it with us. We can do this!* And they did. More than a year after commencing, the graduates have been fabulous contributors. Hannah, Neil, and Joy supported them every step of the way.

While they regularly reached out to check how they were going, Michael, Stuart, and Brett trusted their senior accountants to be leaders in their own right. One of the beautiful observations and lessons from the pandemic has been the blossoming and growth of many young leaders. However, senior leaders and business owners have had to be vulnerable enough to step back and let them lead for the development to occur. The benefit of having a long-term view and that leadership is best when it is shared has proven critical for ProctorMajor and how staff connect with the organisation. In July 2021, the organisation employed another two graduate accountants. Hannah, Neil, and Joy are again trusted to lead and guide them as they start their careers with the business.

Triple role clarity

People understand that the pandemic is a marathon, not a sprint. Co-lead of the inquiry into the pandemic by the World Health Organisation (WHO), Helen Clark, shared that it will be two and half years (towards the end of 2022) before vaccines are appropriately distributed throughout the world. This is not a view that many people were pleased to hear.

In the context of a vaccine with enough time to have its long-term effects checked and double-checked to be safe for most of the global population and then rolled out to all countries, this is proving a realistic target. Vaccines have been developed and released, and changes to the status of some vaccines, such as Astra-Zeneca in Australia, have caused concerns for many people, which has reduced their uptake and slowed the vaccination program.

Therefore, working in a "COVID-normal" world for the medium term is a pragmatic approach. At the time of writing, client after client has expressed how exhausted they were feeling. People are not taking leave because they cannot go anywhere or remain in lockdown, which means they cannot leave home even if they want to. The result is that people have kept working. Online meeting after online meeting is exhausting, but because of the mental model, *"Everyone knows I am working from home. Therefore, I must be available if someone wants me to attend a meeting"* people have continued to make themselves available for meetings that, quite possibly, they did not need to attend.

Leaders need to be proactive in helping their team members focus on the elements of their role that are the most important in the short to medium term. People must be okay with the fact that some aspects of their jobs will not get done. It is not because they are not necessary. It is because they are not needed right now. Equally, team members need to be clear about why what they are doing matters. As Simon Sinek says in his book, *The Infinite Game*, when people know why they are doing what they are doing and how it matters to the larger organisation, it is far easier to find the energy to do the work. In this context, leaders need to help their team members balance doing meaningful work with recognising the extra stresses that exist because of the pandemic. After all, don't you want talented people to be healthy and energised to serve the organisation for the long term?

Daniel Pink referenced this concept another way in his book, *Drive: The Surprising Truth About What Motivates Us*. Pink shared three interdependent elements that drive employee motivation—autonomy, mastery and purpose.

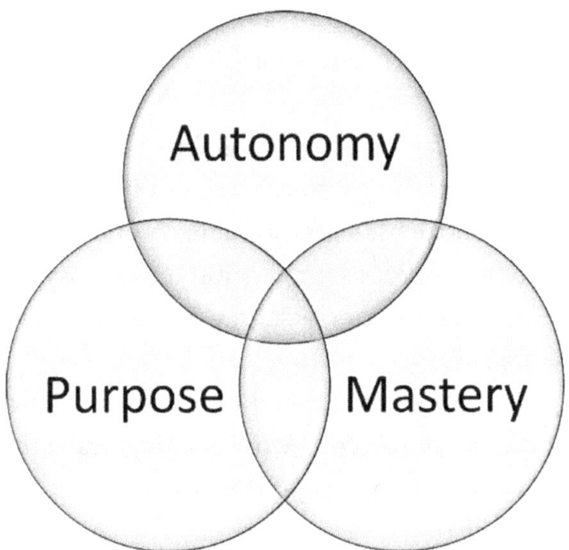

Figure 5: *Employee Motivation Model*

Assuming staff are competent, they require autonomy over their work. While the organisation will dictate **what** needs to be done in a role, employees want autonomy over **how** they do **what** they need to do for their position. The more senior a person becomes, the more autonomy they tend to gain over **both** what they do in their role **and** how they do it. Ensuring staff have as much autonomy as possible is a significant factor in their intrinsic motivation to do their work.

Mastery is the need to improve. Humans like to get better at what they do. Ensuring staff can develop their skills and continue to enhance their strengths is a crucial element for employee intrinsic motivation. Ensuring staff are aware that learning and development continue to be supported by your organisation is essential. Time availability is the primary constraint that people face about their professional development. Ensuring that time is available for staff to learn is crucial if they are to continue developing mastery.

If you have staff that have had a considerable part of their role removed or unable to be performed due to the pandemic, what development opportunities are possible to equip them with the skills you will need as your organisation moves beyond the pandemic? Now may be the perfect time to invest in the development of your people.

Purpose is the desire to do work that makes a difference. No matter what role an employee performs, they want to know that it contributes to something bigger than themselves. When autonomy, mastery, and purpose are present for an employee, they are in the sweet spot that enhances their intrinsic motivation for their role.

Moving forward, enabling employees to have autonomy, mastery and purpose in their roles is a worthwhile aspiration for leaders. Due to the disruption, some functions will change. Some employees may display behaviours associated with the mental model, *"I can't learn new skills."* Remind those employees about the things they did and how they successfully learned to work from home in such a short period. They can learn, and they have proven they can. With help from their leaders, many employees will be able to transition into new roles where necessary.

Can I do this if we don't have a consistent approach to leadership across the organisation?

While completing my research, I spoke with many leaders who believed their organisation practised a "human resource" view of the world. Despite the organisation's lack of a humanistic approach to leadership, they shared examples of their work at a departmental level where they have treated the people they lead as human beings. One leader in local government, and another at a major bank, shared their team engagement scores had dramatically improved throughout the pandemic, despite the overall organisational scores lowering. Unfortunately, for their sake, I can't identify them. They are, however, examples of people who practice the mindset and approaches advocated in these pages, even if the organisation doesn't support them.

It is an arduous journey and more lonely than usual when you lead under these circumstances. A metaphor I reference in these circumstances is you must be like a 130-year-old sea turtle. Your outer shell must be tough and able to repel the constant anti-human demands and behaviours that head toward the department or team you lead. The lack of listening, blaming, and finger-pointing that never seems to end is characteristic of the leaders "above" you in the organisation. But it stops with you. You don't engage in those behaviours. You support the people you lead and protect them from the poor behaviour that you encounter.

No doubt you will identify with the following seemingly simple behaviours. You chose to lead people as "whole people," understanding that each of them has experienced their battles and challenges due to the pandemic and lockdowns. You reached out and checked on them, ensuring they were giving themselves screen-free time and empowering them to make decisions about the work that had to be done, and dropping some of the slightly more discretionary tasks. Where you could, you negotiated with your internal and external customers or stakeholders to change some deadlines associated with your service level agreements. Understanding that team members were doing their jobs and home-schooling, you empowered them to manage their expectations of themselves.

At times, leading your usual high-performers has been challenging throughout the pandemic. You have coached those people to balance their output with everything else in their lives. You listened and empathised and listened and empathised again. You encouraged them not to over-commit and fill their work schedules, understanding that new requests would continue to come in and need to be triaged for importance, which would be okay. You remained conscious of team members burning out and worked with them to minimise this possibility. This doesn't mean that you forgot about productivity. Instead, you balanced productivity with a long-term view, especially when it became clear that the pandemic would not end quickly.

All the while, you ensured you looked after yourself. You practised self-care, providing you with the energy to continue supporting staff, and finally, remained upbeat while not being disconnected from reality – as that can annoy many people! And you did all this while not being sucked into the behaviour of your more senior leaders.

If you recognise yourself in this section, kudos to you! Your efforts to lead the people in your team have been extraordinary, and while you have no doubt experienced times when you have asked yourself, "Does it really make any difference what I do?" The answer is, "Yes!" The people you lead will be grateful for your efforts, and most of them will understand that you have protected them from the broader culture of the organisation.

Behaving in these ways when it isn't part of the organisation's culture can be challenging. But it is doable. Remember, it is not possible to not have a culture. You either get the culture you choose to create, or you get the culture you get. Creating the culture you have decided to make is far better for leaders, followers, and the organisation itself. Of course, sometimes, you can only directly influence the culture you create with your department or team. Either way, "vision" is an essential element for implementing the culture you choose to establish. Empathy, connection, and role clarity matter, not just during the pandemic. These lessons will continue to be powerful beyond the pandemic, as is the power of vision.

$$\diamond$$

Chapter Five:
Vision matters!

"Creative tension" is a concept I first learned from Peter Senge's book, *The Fifth Discipline: The Art & Practice of The Learning Organization.* It happens that Senge first discovered the idea from one of his mentors, Robert Fritz. Fritz is a businessman, a writer, and composer for film. He has worked in both the arts and consulting with Fortune 500 companies most of his life. He first described creative tension in his book, *The Path of Least Resistance.* I find Senge and Fritz's relationship fascinating. Here is Fritz, an artist, mentoring an MIT Sloan School of Management academic and researcher and one of the world's most significant leadership influencers, Senge. The "arts" informing business. How wonderful!

The simplest way to understand creative tension is to consider holding an elastic band between two hands, one above the other. Assuming the hands are apart, tension will exist in the stretched elastic band. Imagine if this is the tension between a vision of the future and your current reality. Your top hand represents your vision or goal, and your bottom hand represents your current reality. There are two ways the tension in the elastic band can be resolved. Either lower your vision or raise your current reality toward your vision. Assuming you want your vision to become

Figure 6: *Creative Tension*

your reality, your vision is then "locked" and causes you to take action to move your current reality toward your vision.

This concept forms a robust structure. Earlier in the book, I shared the smart, hard work example of my daughter Sienna making the impossible possible by being selected in her school's top aerobics team. I could have just as quickly used that story to explain creative tension. By focussing on what she wanted (her vision), Sienna took steps to create that outcome. She recruited friends, did her research to find out what training she should be doing and, importantly, did the training over the six weeks leading into the trials. While her current reality included many reasons she couldn't get selected in the top team, her focus remained on what she wanted rather than what she didn't want. While her actions did not guarantee success, they significantly enhanced the chance of it happening, which it did.

Creative Tension works when you are clear about the vision or goal you want to achieve. The same is true for organisations.

Strategic Plans are an example of documents organisations create to describe their vision. These plans are usually based on three-, five- or ten-year timeframes. Often, they are accompanied by an Action Plan that describes, in detail, what the organisation will do over the first year of implementing the Strategic Plan. As each year concludes, the organisation establishes a new Action Plan to continue the journey. Along the way, the organisation tends to use its Vision Statement, Mission Statement, Values and Action Plan to summarise the tension that the organisation is resolving between its future and current reality.

When used effectively, Creative Tension helps navigate road-blocks to achieving your vision. When Creative Tension is not adequately understood, roadblocks can derail an organisation to the point where its vision becomes irrelevant. The easiest way to resolve the tension is to focus on the organisation's current state. The COVID-19 pandemic is such a roadblock. If an organisation's vision has been weak, or not clear or not shared, then the easiest way to react is to focus on its current real-ity. Which function of an organisation's current reality would draw the most attention when the world's economies have been impacted due to legislated shutdowns by governments worldwide?

Finance.

When an organisation's vision hasn't been "real," it will focus on its current reality. This short-term focus is what was happening before the pandemic but only became noticeable due to it. I suspect this will be one of the greatest lessons for leaders. An old biblical saying is, *"Where there is no vision, the people perish."* (Proverbs 29:18 KJV). Vision matters! The pandemic is just a roadblock around which the organisation needs to navigate if it continues to have a chance to create its vision. Decisions and actions ought to be taken with the vision in focus.

Ask yourself, *"How has our vision influenced our actions throughout the pandemic? How was our vision influencing our actions before the pandemic?"* If you cannot provide examples of how your vision was alive and well before the pandemic, then it is likely that all decisions and actions taken since it started have focussed on your current reality. Concentrating on your current reality during a crisis is what you ought to do. However, if your organisation's vision does not **inform** the context for your actions, actions will be taken based on each person's vision. When personal vision directs the action taken in your current reality, decisions and activities will be inconsistent across an organisation. On the other hand, shared vision is a powerful force that generates consistency in decision-making during a crisis.

In an interview with Karin Volo, chief joy bringer at Evolushen Academy, Bob Chapman, CEO of the Barry Wehmiller Group, was very clear. No employee should lose their job because of an economic downturn. He views it as his responsibility, with his board and senior managers, to create a business model that can sustain downturns. The pandemic has spawned the "mother of all downturns," so the organisation's vision has been tested since February 2020. However, he has consistently said if the company wishes to continue to achieve its vision and growth, it needs to keep its people employed during these difficult times to flourish when good times return. Which they will. Chapman understands that the work he was doing with his board and senior managers before the pandemic came along is benefitting him now.

Australian tech firm Atlassian has recruited more staff than ever in a calendar year throughout 2020. Due to remote work, Atlassian's products and services have been in more demand than ever before. However, rather than simply profiteering from this situation, Atlassian has been proactive in reducing the financial barriers to small organisations accessing its products and services. Owners Mike Cannon-Brookes and Scott Farquhar have been clear that while the pandemic has proven to benefit their company, their value, *"Don't #@!% The Customer,"* must hold, especially when their customer (or in many cases, new customers) are hurting. Vision, mission, and values are, in fact, interdependent. All three are required when making decisions about how to react to the pandemic.

Some of you will discover that the real issue that the pandemic has surfaced, highlighted by your reaction to it, is that your vision, mission, and values were not "alive" before February 2020. Yes, they were printed on the walls of your offices and in your annual reports, but they weren't alive in the sense of informing day-to-day decisions. Your vision has been to maintain financial viability. Period. We do live with the economic fact that organisations need finances to survive. However, if you have operated from the perspective that growth is constant and forever moving upward, you wouldn't have prepared for a financial "rainy day." The never-ending pressure for this year's financial reports to read better than last year has created a tension that has caused many leaders to be driven to make decisions for the sake of the short term, with little or no regard for what that may mean for the long term.

As we saw earlier, employee engagement is paramount for long-term organisational success. A lack of understanding of this relationship has caused many leaders to reduce headcount as early as possible, to "save the bottom line." Unfortunately, these actions have been necessary in many instances because the companies were never prepared for a downturn, even though history is full of their occurrences (think the global financial crisis of 2008, as just one example). From an economic perspective, companies have had to make these cuts to save some jobs. As we move forward, the lesson from Bob Chapman is powerful. Can your business model sustain the next downturn?

Roadblocks help you to recognise your vision is missing

MONSU Caulfield is the student association that serves undergraduate students at the Caulfield Campus for Monash University in Melbourne, Australia. The pandemic caused significant disruption to the tertiary sector in Australia due to international students not being able to enter Australia due to the international border closure. Many thousands of students withdrew from their courses or have continued to study online. The once-vibrant Caulfield campus became a ghost town overnight and remained in limbo. Despite never giving up, the efforts from the team of staff and available student representatives, in addition to the efforts from university staff, have had little impact on students physically attending campus (when the restrictions have allowed this to happen).

Lyn Nye, general manager of MONSU Caulfield, and Caitlyn Dunne, 2020 president, recognised early in the pandemic that the organisation didn't have a clear vision to guide its decision-making. Notions existed in individual staff and student representative's minds, but they were loose and not coordinated and driving the organisation. Lyn and Caitlyn were aware that the downturn in student enrolments would immediately affect the organisation's revenue. As a precaution, they made tough decisions to manage their expenses. They included staff in conversations about their predicament, and with support from them, agreed to limit each person's workload to the critical work associated with keeping the organisation afloat.

As soon as they had ensured they had financial viability for the foreseeable future, primarily due to the prudent financial management of the organisation occurring well before the pandemic, they decided to rectify their lack of a compelling vision and put together a team to develop a strategic plan. The development of the strategic plan occurred 100% online over five months and was ratified by the new executive council early in 2021. It will continue to be reviewed on an annual basis.

As is typical with the creative process associated with developing a vision, as staff and student representatives engaged and contributed to its development, they found themselves inspired to take actions that were moving them toward their picture of the future. One clear example is their strategic goal relating to the organisation's environmental impact. Despite the disruption to their services continuing into 2021, the organisation has made considerable progress with its environmental goals. The positivity

that has flowed from the project has helped the organisation con-
tend with the ongoing challenges that the pandemic has inflicted
on its other, essential operations.

Use the disruption to revisit your vision

A critical benefit of any disruption is that it creates an opportunity to ask yourself, *"Is our vision what we want?"* A vision does
not have to be set in stone. Instead, it gathers clarity over time.
Sometimes, you may discover that what you thought you wanted
isn't what you want at all. You find out that you want something
different, which is fine. Readjust and change direction to get you
on the path to creating your new vision.

Often, you discover that you **do** want to achieve your vision
despite what is happening in your current reality. This is one of
the most beneficial aspects of disruption. While the disruption
may affect your current situation, when it helps you re-affirm
where you want to go, it gives you the energy to identify and then
implement the required strategies to get you there.

Gareth Kent, director at Preston Rowe Paterson (PRP),
Geelong, Warrnambool, and Mt Gambier in Australia, recognised
that his companies' vision needed refreshing. While the company
vision was relevant to him, he doubted whether it was front of
mind for the staff in the organisation. Demand for residential,
commercial, and agricultural property valuations skyrocketed,
as did the requirement for valuations provided for family law
purposes. He had recruited more staff, and everyone was busier
than ever. Gareth engaged me to work with all staff to refresh the
company vision. Over three months of interaction and feedback,
an updated vision, mission, and values statement was released.
Notably, the new statement isn't just a set of brand new, shiny

words on posters. It has been directly referenced and used for decision-making. The recently formed leadership team have been regularly challenged to provide examples of the vision-in-action, and those sessions have continued throughout 2021. In a mid-year session, one of the youngest members of the leadership team shared a challenge he faced outside work. One of the updated values is "Caring and communicating." Every leader listened with 100% attention when he shared his story. He explained that he was confident in sharing his situation with the rest of the leadership team because of the care and support he had received from Gareth and the rest of the directors. One of the leaders, a confessed, "hard-nosed numbers guy," said, *"Wow, that conversation was raw. And that's exactly the sort of team I want to be part of. At some point, something will happen to all of us, and we will need care and support! This is about more than work and the numbers."*

From October 2020 through June 2021, Gareth's business experienced six record months of growth and recruited another five staff. Vision matters, and PRP Geelong, Warrnambool and Mt Gambier is proof of the power it can generate. Equally, vision can create frustration which is typical for all leaders.

How to overcome the frustration that comes with a vision

Lyn Nye is frustrated. Her organisation is far from achieving the vision created by its strategic plan developed in the last half of 2020. Lyn's frustration is standard and comes with the territory of being a leader. This is the "tension" in the term, "creative tension." The nature of leadership is that the future you want to create is more evident to you than your followers. The gap is as apparent to you as the nose on your face. But the picture of the future your vision paints, and the assessment of the gap between it and your current reality, isn't as apparent to everyone else. At least, that is how it can feel when you are "at the top." It often feels lonely. That is why working with your leadership team, as Lyn has, is essential to enable them to share in the vision. And so is taking stock and celebrating the progress of your current reality.

As the "bottom of the elastic band" moves toward your vision, notice the successes you create along the way. Celebrate them. Use the celebrations and recognition of progress as the catalyst for smart, hard work that is required to progress your journey.

Following strict guidelines, Gareth, and the team from PRP Geelong, Warrnambool and Mt Gambier celebrated Christmas in July. Despite a lockdown causing a postponement to the function, most staff and their partners were in attendance, many of them having travelled hundreds of kilometres. At the event, Gareth went to great lengths to recognise all staff and their partners for their work and the personal challenges they had overcome throughout the previous 16 months to serve their customers. Marriages, childbirths, qualification achievements and the company's success were all celebrated.

The event could have easily been placed in the too-hard basket. And it was hard to organise, given COVID restrictions and repeated lockdowns. But Gareth and his team persisted because recognising the company's progress and everyone's contribution to it, including their partners and families, was too important not to celebrate. The conversations between staff and their partners were a joy to witness. And it is to the quality of all your conversations that we now focus your attention.

Chapter Six:
The quality of your conversations matters

Water is to fish, as conversations are to humans. When a fish is caught, and the angler unhooks it and places it on the boat's floor, what does the fish do? It flips and flops, gasping for water. It does everything within its

Figure 7: *Water is to fish as conversations are to humans*

power to get back into the water. The fish has no awareness of the importance of water to its survival until it is no longer in it.

Similarly, humans go from one conversation to the next, effectively unaware of the importance of conversational skills. Consider yourself. How many conversations have you had today? Were you conscious of the skills you were using in those conversations, or did you participate as you usually do?

No doubt you have participated in communication courses and workshops and may have read books on the topic. Yet, there is every probability that you have participated in today's conversations from a sub-conscious position, effectively **unaware** of how you are conversing.

What if you recognised that conversation skills are equally critical to your success, as water is to fish? Might you see the importance of highly developed conversation skills differently?

If we assume that the quality of our conversations matters, imagine if the quality is poor. What effect might that have on your decisions? Given your choices direct your actions, how effective are your actions likely to be? Over time, what long-term impact will your actions have on your performance?

The most likely outcome is that if the quality of your conversations is poor, which means you are making poor decisions, you will be taking the wrong actions and negatively impacting performance over time. What if you invested in improving the quality of your conversations? Over time, what positive impact could that have on all your life roles? As a leader, what benefits might the organisation receive if you improve the quality of your conversations?

Warren Bennis, Daniel Goleman, and James O'Toole identified "truth to power" as an essential element for organisational success in their book, *Transparency*. Organisations have inherent power imbalances. The more senior a person becomes, the more power they possess to make decisions that affect other people. Having power over others can negatively affect the quality of your conversations with them. If you do not have well-developed conversational skills, people with less power will likely tell you what they think you want to hear. You use this false information as part of your decision-making process, which means your decisions won't be as good as they could have been. Most likely, you won't realise when people aren't telling you their truth because you won't have developed the skills to increase the probability of them telling you the truth. You have no doubt heard the saying, *"Don't shoot the messenger!"* This saying arose because so many messengers were killed by kings and queens when the king or queen didn't like the message they were receiving. Messengers were literally killed!

While today people know they won't be killed for delivering a message their leader may not like, they would prefer someone else to deliver the message. Their lizard brain kicks in, and they take the safe road and tell their leader only what they think the leader wants to hear. In most organisations, "truth to power" is far lower than it would be if the conversational skills of leaders were better developed. The benefit of developing these skills is exponential.

Despite several decades of research, it wasn't until Julia Rozovsky's Project Aristotle at Google that Professor Amy Edmondson's research was made famous. When researching the fundamental requirements for creating a high-performing team, Rozovsky and her colleagues discovered five crucial elements. One of those elements provided the fertile soil upon which the other four elements benefitted. The five elements were:

1. **Psychological safety:** Team members must be comfortable in taking risks and speaking their minds. They need to know that their team members will support their actions and not ridicule them. Everyone on the team must feel like they won't be made examples of if something goes wrong.
2. **Dependability:** Everyone needs to contribute to the best of their ability and deliver high-quality work. They must do this within agreed parameters. Dependability means that they can count on each other to do their job.
3. **Structure and clarity:** Clear direction and goals are vital. Recall, "Clarity is Queen!" Everyone needs to understand what part they play on the team. Everyone on the team also needs to know how they should get their job done to help the team succeed.
4. **Meaning of work:** Google's researchers seemed to find that individual personal satisfaction in the job they were performing was also a key element in the team's success.
5. **Impact of work:** How does the work that people are doing benefit the company? Team members want to feel that they are not wasting their time when doing things.

Psychological safety is the element upon which the other four are nourished, and Professor Edmondson has advocated its importance since 1999. According to Edmondson, psychological safety is naturally low, and the low level is reinforced through the organisational hierarchy. Neuroscience teaches us that humans require hierarchy as part of our natural mammalian instincts. The gap that status differences create in an organisation increases the probability that staff will not speak their truth. The risks are simply too high.

As a leader, the more you understand this phenomenon, the more you can deliberately increase the psychological safety of people in the organisation. One simple, yet powerful tactic, is to have members from different layers of the hierarchy learn together. This tactic is precisely what Daniel Auld from Eric Jones Stairbuilding has done.

Daniel has repeatedly let the other four leaders in the leadership program know that he is learning, just like them while he is in the room. He has worked hard to listen and has encouraged the frontline leaders to speak their truth, even if they are concerned he may not like what they tell him. Over 20 months, the degree to

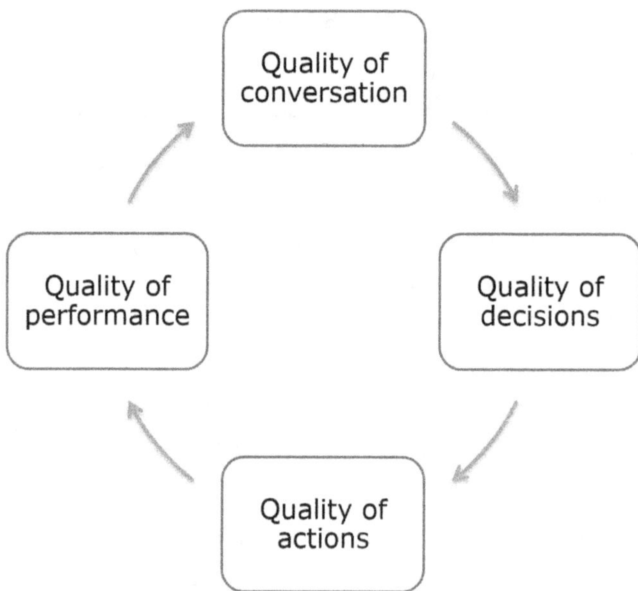

Figure 8: *Quality Conversation Model*

which all five leaders have conducted high-quality conversations has been a pleasure to witness.

Developing your conversational skills are essential if you want to be an effective leader. Below are the characteristics of the vital skills for conducting high-quality conversations.

High-quality conversation characteristics

Listen for understanding

The first is listening. You must listen. But it is not listening for agreement. It is listening for understanding. You must listen to check that you genuinely understand what the "other" is saying. A specific form of active listening, where we use a technique from neurolinguistic programming (NLP), is to deliberately listen for the **nouns** or naming words that the people we're talking with say, in addition to the **verbs** or **action phrases** that are said.

When you start to practice this technique, you will notice that people use many nouns and verbs or action phrases when they speak. You're not going to be able to identify all of them. What you try to do is listen for the ones that seem like they're the most powerful. You listen for these nouns or naming words and verbs or action phrases when you're consciously listening. Then, as you participate in the conversation, as much as you possibly can, you work those same nouns, verbs, and action phrases into the conversation. Do not change them. If someone incorrectly names something, don't correct them at the start. Use the same noun they use. If they say "apples" instead of "apple," then you say "apples."

When you listen in this way, you continually provide the other person with evidence that you are listening to them. This tactic is even more critical when you're working with people for whom English might be another language. Don't correct them. Just listen. When English is a second, third or more language, people can be easier to listen to than when English is their first language. Why? Due to their smaller vocabulary, they use fewer nouns, verbs, and action phrases, making the key ones easier to hear. There are times you might ask, eventually in your relationship, *"Would you like some advice on better ways to say things?"* They'll likely accept your offer. At the start of your relationship, continue to use the nouns, verbs, and action phrases they say to give them the evidence you are listening to them. Let them complete what they're saying. Listen without interruption.

Please recall the previous section about your brain and how it works. Remember the section about mindfulness and the techniques to help calm yourself. There will be times when something triggers your automatic emotional responses. As your emotional states increases, what do you think happens to your ability to listen?

Thousands of people in the workshops I conduct have agreed that the most probable outcome is that your ability to be an effective listener decreases under these circumstances. You know what I am talking about. No doubt, you have experienced someone else lose their cool, and it becomes evident to everyone that they are not listening to a single word anyone else is saying. As a leader, do you think this outcome is beneficial or a hindrance?

I am not aware of a single person suggesting this outcome is beneficial to the leader. Once you notice your emotions, use that as a trigger to activate one of the techniques recommended by mindfulness experts Associate Professor Craig Hassed and Dr

Richard Chambers. Faster than you may expect, you will be able to bring your attention back to the skills of listening. None of us is perfect. You will get this wrong from time to time, but when you notice yourself getting it wrong, catch yourself, immediately re-commence these listening techniques and improve the quality of the conversation.

Ask high-quality questions

Imagine if while you're listening for nouns, verbs and action phrases, your attention is equally focussed on, *"What question will help me to progress this conversation? What's the most powerful question I can ask that will contribute to progressing this conversation?"*

Notice, your focus is **not**, *"What's the most powerful thing I can say? What's the most powerful statement I can make to show how smart I am?"*

High-quality questions are genuine, which means that you are comfortable with whatever answer you receive. When my 10-year-old son, at 8 pm last night, came and asked me if he could have a chocolate bar, which he already had in his hand, and I said "No." He got rather upset with that answer. Was his question genuine? Was he open to whatever answer I gave him? No, he wasn't. He only wanted one answer. His question was not genuine.

Think about the questions you have asked today? How many of them were genuine questions? Were you 100% open to whatever answers you received? Think about it.

In my experience, a very high proportion of your questions will have been non-genuine questions. Like my 10-year-old son, you had pre-determined answers you were seeking, and if you did not get the answers you liked, you would have signalled your displeasure in some form or other.

When asking a genuine question, you do not know the answer. This is why you are asking the question. A tactic I recommend is to be open to *more than one correct answer*.

Genuine questions are not "lazy" questions. Imagine you have a mentee. While the mentee was aware they ought to prepare questions for sessions with their mentor, imagine they didn't prepare for meeting with you. In the session, they start asking lots of questions. On the surface, this may seem consistent with what I am suggesting. However, the mentee could have easily discovered the answers to their questions before your session if they had completed some research. As a result of their research, more considered questions would have surfaced, and you could have spent your time in the session exploring these powerful questions instead of the "low-hanging fruit."

A lazy question is when you have not done some smart, hard work. You have not taken responsibility for your questions. You are placing the responsibility for your questions on the person's shoulders to whom you are asking the question.

I appreciate that the practice I am recommending is not easy. This is why it is a game-changer because when you master it, you have the skill to positively influence the quality of every conversation within which you are a participant.

Four questions for the people you lead

Imagine if every person you are leading had absolute role clarity. They know what their responsibilities are and how they will be measured against those key responsibilities. What if these measures aligned with high-performance? What if each team member was clear about what high performance for their key responsibilities looked like at the start of the year?

Without referencing their position description, do you believe most team members could articulate their key responsibilities as if they were at a dinner party? Could they say the list of things for which they are responsible, and, if pressed, could they just as quickly explain how they know how they are performing? How likely is it that whatever your team members said would match what you would expect them to say?

From my experience, most people have between three to six key responsibilities. The more senior you are, the more high-level those responsibilities become. While it is possible to have more than six key responsibilities, I have found that this breeds the circumstances where they are replaced by at least two people when they leave the organisation. Either the person was doing the job of two people, or significant aspects of their key responsibilities were ignored.

The four questions are:
1. How are you going with your key responsibilities?
2. How are you nurturing the key relationships you need to foster to deliver on your key responsibilities?
3. What help do you need from me to achieve your key responsibilities or nurture your key relationships effectively?
4. How are you going progressing with your agreed development activities?

How are you going with your key responsibilities?

For each key responsibility, both you and the member of your team need to be able to answer the question, *"How do I know*

I am doing a great good job for this key responsibility?" Notice the question is not asking, *"How do I get a pass mark for this key responsibility?"*

Interestingly, most of the education system teaches people that a grade of 50% is a pass. I am not sure I have ever seen a performance level of 50% be satisfactory in the workplace. Imagine if you only performed at 50%. How long do you think you would keep your job? Often, more than one measure is required, but they need to be straightforward. If measures are not clear, they're not helpful. They can be quantitative or qualitative measures. Over time, people have said to me, *"Gary, we sat down, but we can't work out what the measures might be for one of the key responsibilities. What should we do?"*

Sometimes, the leader and the follower need to regularly sit down and agree to discuss performance against that specific key responsibility. The two of you will decide whether the team member is on track or not. This decision will be the qualitative measure you will use for that key responsibility. Remember, keep it simple. Please access the website at **www.disruptionleadershipmatters.com/resources** to obtain a spreadsheet that will enable you to identify your key responsibilities and relationships. Please watch the short video that explains how to use the template.

How are you nurturing the key relationships you need to foster to deliver on your key responsibilities?

After identifying your key responsibilities and clarifying how they will be measured, it is vital to consider the various relationships you will need to foster to deliver on your key commitments. While all relationships are meaningful, I urge you to consider the relationships that will directly and significantly impact your ability to deliver on your key responsibilities. The following people or groups of people need to be considered:

- Your manager
- Anyone who reports to you
- Anyone in another department for who you are a customer of their work, or they are a customer of your work
- Anyone outside your organisation with whom you are required to work so that you can achieve your objectives. These may include:
    o   Contractors
    o   Suppliers
    o   Customers
    o   Partners

Marshall Goldsmith, regularly regarded as the "World's #1 Executive Coach," suggests that the average number of critical relationships on your list is 18. From my 14 years of coaching, I agree with Goldsmith that this is a reasonable number. *"That's a lot of relationships I have to nurture,"* I hear you say.

Yes, it is. Depending on your role, this number may be a lot higher. Gareth Kent, Director at PRP Geelong, Warrnambool and Mt Gambier, currently has 127 people on his list. Do you think the pattern with which Gareth contacts the people on his list is the same for everyone or unique to each relationship?

The pattern of contact is unique. With his direct reports, it is multiple times per day. It is also multiple times per day with other staff in the organisation, while there is less frequent contact for other team members, depending on their role. Some of his contacts are on a weekly pattern, while others are on monthly, quarterly, or bi-annual patterns. It all depends on the relationship and the frequency and type of contact required to foster high-quality relationships. The important lesson is that Gareth is **aware** of the relationships he must nurture and their associated contact pattern.

For most staff, their list will include their manager, team members, colleagues from other departments they interact with when completing their tasks, and external people such as customers, suppliers, contractors, and consultants. Again, precisely who is on their list and the frequency of contact will depend on their role.

Answering this question enables staff to see the connection between their work and other people. It also helps them see the tangible link between achieving their key responsibilities and their relationships with people.

What help do you need from me to achieve your key responsibilities or nurture your key relationships effectively?

Your role is to support your staff to do their job to the best of their ability. Your job is **NOT** to do their job. This question is not about you taking responsibility away from the members of your team. Instead, it is about identifying how you can help them. They may discover they have some technical gaps in their capacity to perform their role. Your support would include finding the resources, monetary or otherwise, so they can have access to whatever they need to close this gap.

Similarly, they may have challenges with some of their key relationships. Depending on the issue, it may be appropriate for you to leverage an existing relationship with someone, so they don't have to start a new one or repair a damaged one. On other occasions, such action may detract from their role, so it may be more appropriate to work with them to develop the new relationship or find ways to repair it. Either way, you are conscious of the support you are providing and equally aware of how your actions are helping or hindering them perform their role to the best of their ability.

How are you going progressing with your agreed development activities?

There are generally three valid reasons for an organisation to support the development of an employee.

1. The development activity is directly related to closing some technical gaps that are specific to doing the work associated with their key responsibilities.
2. The development activity is directly related to developing skills that will enable them to nurture their key relationships more effectively.
3. The development activity is related to the career aspirations of the employee.

What would you do if you had a team member whose key responsibilities changed on 31st March 2022? If you assume the staff member's responsibilities, measures and critical relationships were identified at the start of the year; you would assess their performance against those agreements until 31st March 2022. Usually, most of the person's role would remain, with one or two additional responsibilities added. Having gained clarity about the staff member's role at the start of the year, both of you will be able to negotiate the changes necessary to ensure the new responsibilities are feasible. Sometimes, it will be evident that a previous key responsibility needs to be removed to facilitate the new responsibility being included in the person's role from 1st April.

The new responsibility will require its measures to be identified, as will any new relationships that need nurturing. Remember, always keep the criteria as simple as possible. When you get to the end of the year, you need to measure the performance from 1st April to 31st December and add it to the results you identified for 1st January to 31st March.

No doubt you are thinking things never go this smoothly. And you would be correct. They don't. It may be the end of April before the changes are clarified, which means the process can be a bit messy. However, a little bit of a mess for a month is far better than a massive problem that grows over the next eight months because you reduced role clarity from 1st April.

How regularly should these conversations occur?

Too often, organisational performance appraisal systems require these types of conversations to occur three times per year. One at the start of the year, one mid-year and another at the end of the year (often in conjunction with the conversation about the beginning of the following year). If you are serious about role clarity, then three times a year is nowhere near enough. I strongly recommend you conduct these conversations at least eight times per year with each direct report.

The conversations do not need to be a formal meeting. You could have them while walking to your local café or travelling alongside each other in a car on the way to a meeting or job (when it is COVID-19 safe to do so). Or, while playing table tennis! Why not! What matters is that both you and the people you lead are clear about what their job is and what doing a great job looks like. The more you can support that happening, the more successful you are as a leader, the more successful the people you lead are in their roles, and the more successful the organisation is in attaining its goals. The outcomes are worth the effort required to achieve them. Over time, these conversations become embedded in your culture and will give you long-lasting benefits.

Let people finish speaking

I am constantly amazed at how often colleagues speak over the top of one another. From my experience in observing thousands of workplace conversations, who do you think is the most likely to talk over the top of other team members? What role do you think that person holds? If you guessed it was the leader, you would be correct. Do you believe leaders name themselves as the most interrupting person on their team? The answer is no, they don't. Yet, they are the most likely person in a group to interrupt and talk over the top of team members.

Let's highlight this point again. Leaders are the most likely people to interrupt and talk over the top of another team member, yet the leader is unaware of this behaviour. If you are a leader and regularly talk over the top of your team members, how do you think this affects their view of you as a listener?

They will believe you are a poor listener. Why? Because talking over the top of people is a sure way to tell them that your ears are painted on and don't work! We have two ears and one mouth for a good reason. Use your ears and listen. You will never regret being known as a good listener.

Figure 9: *Two ears and one mouth*

Share the floor

Sharing the floor means you hear from everyone. You allow everyone to speak, and you get comfortable with silence. That can be a real challenge for some people. Silence is essential for some people, particularly for our more introverted folk, or people for whom English is another language, who may need time for translation, to have time to think. However, when the extroverted folks get uncomfortable with silence, they jump in and fill the silence, which detracts from the quality of the conversation.

Be explicit about the fact that you want to hear from everyone in your team. Psychological safety results in all team members feeling safe enough to speak their minds. When psychological safety is present, you would observe all team members throughout your journey, contributing somewhat equal amounts to the collective conversation. This doesn't mean that in a single meeting, all team members would speak equal amounts. Instead, when you consider all the one-on-one and team-based conversations throughout your team's journey, the overall contribution to the exchanges is somewhat similar from all team members.

New possibilities are possible

The outcome of a high-quality conversation is that new possibilities are at least *possible*. It's not, "We used to do it this way, so we're always going to do it that way in the future." Instead, you explore possibilities. Consider this question. If a new possibility is possible, does that mean we will always do them?

No, it doesn't mean we will always do them. Through your exploration, you might discover that the new possibility isn't the best idea. That's okay. At least you allowed yourself to explore it, and because of that exploration, the better idea does come to the surface, and you can potentially implement that idea. It is the freedom to explore that provides the most incredible value of high-quality conversations. And, as you read earlier, increased diversity enhances the generation of ideas that lead to innovation.

Does exploring a new possibility mean that you must change whatever it is that you are doing? No. It may be that what you are doing continues to be the best way to do it at this time. But you were open to the exploration, nonetheless. High-quality conversations don't lock you into change. Instead, they allow the continuous flow of life to be present, so you have the chance to change things for the better if that is right for what you are striving to achieve. High-quality conversations validate a sense of curiosity that will permeate your culture and become the usual way of talking with each other. Innovations will occur because of some

of the possibilities that high-quality conversations have enabled.
I'm yet to work with a single organisation that doesn't desire innovation, which is why deliberately enhancing the quality of your
conversations is essential.

I am an advocate for enhancing this competence at all levels
of your organisation. But it must start with you, the leader. You
have likely ignored this set of skills because you believe you are
already a master of conversation. Suppose you are; kudos to you
and the work you have done to be an influential conversation-
alist. However, in most situations, you and your colleagues have
work to do. Take action to improve your conversational competence deliberately. You will discover nothing will be more influential on your leadership and your organisation's performance than
improving the quality of your conversations.

Chapter Seven:
Don't just read - take action!

n the introduction to his most recent book, *The Unexpected Learning Moment*, Garry Ridge, CEO of WD-40, shares that he "met" Ken Blanchard when he was 28 years old. Garry has been an avid reader all his life, and he first "met" Ken Blanchard via reading his books. I suspect you are similar, as you would not be reading this book if you weren't. I hope you feel as if you have "met" me!

Reading is an essential step for learning. But it isn't learning by itself. Recall The Knowing-Doing Gap. While you have been reading, your mind will have been triggering ideas for taking action to improve your leadership. In 1995, when I started reading *The Fifth Discipline* by Peter Senge, it took more than six months to complete the book. It wasn't because I was a slow reader or kept putting the book down for long periods. It was because I was doing my best to put what I was learning into practice. As I was reading the book, I was doing my best to "do" the book. At that time, I wasn't aware of The Knowing-Doing Gap. Still, my newfound awareness that I had mental models directly influencing my behaviour caused me to want to consciously take action rather than be subject to my seemingly automatic behaviours.

Taking action is incredibly important if you desire improvement. However, acting without any form of feedback is likely to limit your progress. Feedback that is regular, timely and honest plays an integral role in your development. You indeed can raise your self-awareness and emotional intelligence to the point where you can provide feedback to yourself. If this is the only form of feedback you receive, you will miss meaningful opportunities for improvement that your colleagues could provide.

From my experience, the leaders and teams that make the most progress toward creating a culture of honesty and accountability, both of which are significant drivers for high-performance, practise in-person, face-to-face feedback. Think about it. How active are you in seeking feedback for your performance and behaviour? Given the power imbalance between yourself and the team you lead and the natural tendency for humans to accept hierarchy, what are you doing to help your colleagues provide feedback to yourself and their colleagues? How are you helping them recognise that when you provide feedback, it is only equal to the input provided by their peers?

The Tokyo Olympic Games have concluded, and many people I work with have shared how pleasant a distraction the sporting events were to watch and 'escape' from the reality of the pandemic, even if it was just for a little while, each day. I doubt a single athlete who competed at the games does not have a coach who offers them constant feedback. Which raises an interesting question. How do you seek and receive feedback?

Anonymous surveys have a place from a feedback perspective, but on their own, I believe they create more problems than they resolve. The anonymous data can identify patterns, but the context and detail from the examples are often missing. The feedback recipient is left guessing what it all means and wondering who said what about them. A better form of feedback includes face-to-face feedback. You can compare patterns from the anonymous feedback with face-to-face feedback and identify essential behaviours that are assisting or hindering your effectiveness as a leader. The mere suggestion of face-to-face feedback from leaders and peers alike often puts fear into the heart of potential recipients. However, in-person feedback is essential if you are serious about feedback and being true to your espoused culture. As a leader, I strongly urge you to act and seek feedback.

How to seek regular feedback from colleagues

When attempting a new behaviour or wanting to do more of a behaviour that you know works, seek out three or four colleagues. These could be your manager, your peers or the team members who report to you. Be open and vulnerable enough to let them know you are attempting to improve or change a behaviour. Be explicit about the behaviour change you are seeking. Ask them to provide you with discreet, timely re-enforcement when they see you behave as you intend, as well as when you slip and act in a manner that hinders your performance as a leader. Let them know that you are serious about behaviour change and you are aware that you may take some time to push through the learning curve. In other words, you have realistic expectations about how long it will take to master your new behaviours.

A simple example may be that you know you talk over the top of people and need to stop doing it. You ask three or four of your colleagues to observe you and to provide you with feedback. In our current world, it may be a quick message after an online meeting that cites an explicit example where you caught yourself and let someone continue speaking after you had interrupted them. Or the feedback may tell you that you continued to talk over the top of your colleagues and offer you an explicit example. If you do catch yourself talking over the top of someone, I encourage you to say, *"I'm sorry. Please continue."*

Assuming you are serious about the behaviours you intend to improve; this method is very effective in ensuring that you maintain a high level of awareness of how you are acting and whether that is consistent with what you want. Utilising the same method, you could provide your peers with a little more structure. After explaining your desire to improve and seek feedback from them, ask them to let you know what behaviours they believe you should keep doing, stop doing and start doing. When I support leaders to utilise this method, they are surprised and often humbled by what they are reminded to keep doing. Usually, there is one behaviour they either need to stop doing or start doing. In addition to the ones they ought to keep doing, they can make all the difference to significantly improved leadership outcomes.

A structure for face-to-face feedback

Earlier, you met Daniel, Joe, Sam, Matt, and Stefano from Eric Jones Stairbuilding Group. They are practical people who make magnificent staircases. In March 2021, as they progressed through their leadership development journey, I offered them the opportunity to rotate through a process where they would receive face-to-face feedback from each other. To a person, they agreed to do it while acknowledging a level of apprehension about the process.

To keep things simple, the example below focuses on face-to-face feedback. It is best if this can be conducted in person.

However, online versions are also possible. The process commences with a reminder that the team is providing feedback to their colleague to help them be the best they can be in that role for the organisation. Any input that doesn't directly relate to their role for the business is not relevant and has no place in the process. We also discuss humour. Like other cultures, part of the Australian culture includes using humour to relieve tension. The challenge with sprinkling humour throughout a feedback process is that it can create confusion for the recipient. *"Are they serious about what they just told me, or are they joking?"*

The person who is to receive the feedback moves to another room and prepares their responses to the following questions:

- What do I think they will unanimously tell me I should keep doing?
- What do I think they will unanimously tell me I should stop doing?
- What do I think they will unanimously tell me I should start doing?

While the person receiving the feedback is preparing, their colleagues discuss and take notes on what they **unanimously** believe their peer should keep doing, stop doing and start doing. The purpose of providing unanimous feedback is to eliminate input that may be personal or based on a grudge. Any feedback that is not unanimous should be shared independently of this process.

When both groups are ready, the person receiving the feedback joins their colleagues. A whiteboard is used to record responses. Everyone is reminded to leave humour out of the process (you would be amazed how many times people need reminding of this rule as nervous tension bubbles to the surface). When the team provides their feedback, if required, the receiver can ask questions to clarify what has been said. The receiver's clarifying questions are to ensure they understand what they have been told. The questions are not about being defensive or trying to reach an agreement. Instead, they are about understanding.

After the receiver has heard all the feedback and understood it (they do not have to agree with it, they just have to understand what they have been told) and it has been recorded on the whiteboard, the receiver shares what they believed they were going to be told for each of the three questions. Again, team members can ask questions to clarify their understanding of what the receiver is saying. When everyone agrees they understand what has been said, the entire team consider the patterns that may be present from both sets of data on the whiteboard. A conversation is held to identify any actions that the recipient determines they will act upon as an outcome from the feedback, and who will support them in implementing those behaviours is identified.

As each Eric Jones Stairbuilding Group leader has taken their turn to receive feedback, I have acknowledged their courage and willingness to be open to being vulnerable. You might not associate vulnerability with tradespeople, but here they are, being as vulnerable as any group of leaders I have ever worked with. It is all because they genuinely want to improve. None of them is a perfect leader, and they never will be. That isn't the goal. Instead, it is about enhancing their leadership skills over time and trusting their peers to help them along the journey, and no one can ask more than that!

It is essential to note that Daniel is a participant in the process. In one session, Daniel offered to be the scribe and provide feedback to the recipient. No doubt you could imagine that when the business owner relays the unanimous feedback to you, it might hold more weight than if one of the other leaders did it. We discussed this issue numerous times throughout the journey. All leaders genuinely understand that Daniel participates in the process because he is learning, just like them. Achieving this collective mindset takes time, and it doesn't mean that Daniel isn't directive in the day-to-day operations of the business when he needs to be. Still, when all the leaders are learning together, they are genuine peers irrespective of their title. Daniel, Joe, Matt, Sam, and Stefano are genuinely learning together, and it is a pleasure to witness.

You can download the worksheets and process for conducting this type of face-to-face feedback from **www.disruptionleadershipmatters.com/resources**.

What happens next? As the world moves from attempting to suppress the virus to living with it, what will be the long-term effects of the pandemic and the disruption it caused? What has changed forever? What are the questions that do not yet have answers? As a leader, what do these questions mean for you?

$$\diamond$$

Chapter Eight:
Moving beyond the pandemic

I have been extremely fortunate that several leaders have shared their thoughts about what the disruption means for their industry, the changes that are here to stay, at least for the foreseeable future, and the unanswered questions and challenges.

Marcus Pitt, financial advisor, Deloitte, Singapore, shares that one change that will remain is the flexibility to work from both home and the office. Recently, the firm's Indonesian office in Jakarta trialled satellite offices rather than centralised offices in the CBD. For example, the firm established east and west offices, each approximately 15 kilometres from the CBD. While staff will continue to work in a hybrid model, when they go to the office, they will choose to go to a location that is a shorter commute, rather than going into the CBD. This will likely be the model for huge cities like Jakarta. While the extra 15 kilometres may not seem like much, it can equate to saving up to two hours of commuting each day in a city such as Jakarta, which is highly congested with traffic. What this means for traditional CBDs is one of the unanswered questions that many leaders will need to resolve as the world moves beyond the pandemic.

Thailand's CP Group CEO Supachai Chearavanont believes that the success of public-private partnerships throughout the pandemic shows the true success of governments and private enterprises working together and that collaborating for the benefit of society is going to be an essential lesson from the pandemic. His company has launched "CP 4.0," which uses technological innovation to move the agro-business into the 21st Century. Supachai is challenging the leaders in his business to use technology, data, artificial intelligence, and e-commerce to ensure CP Group delivers healthier food for consumers, producing carbon-neutral and zero-waste outcomes by 2030. The ability of the organisation to pivot to working from home and using the available technology to sustain operations throughout the pandemic provides Supachai with the confidence to set this bold vision.

Supachai advocates that stock exchanges will move to demand organisations report their progress toward zero emissions targets. Such a change would represent a structural shift in the thinking behind how world markets operate, providing a solution that imbeds the relationship between operations and environmental sustainability.

Rob Clayton, managing director of Nutrien Ag Solutions Australia, believes that the disruption has catalysed a new approach to workplace flexibility that represents a shift in thinking from the executive. Empirical evidence from 2020 and 2021 indicates that working from home is both possible and productive. Staff have logged on when they otherwise would have been commuting. While Rob doesn't believe working from home will continue at the same levels that lockdowns have forced, it will remain. It has already allowed Nutrien to access a whole new cohort of employees, dramatically improving the diversity and inclusion of Nutrien's workforce.

On the other hand, flexibility poses a challenge. If staff rarely come into face-to-face contact, how will mentoring and the development of the desired culture occur? If not enough flexibility is available, then the benefits from attracting new talent to the organisation will be lost. Trials have already commenced attempting to resolve this challenge, and a lot of learning is ahead of the organisation as it grapples with finding a solution for its workforce.

Another critical lesson for the organisation is the importance of its digital offering to customers. Due to retail stores being allowed to remain open due to their essential service status, Nutrien realised the fragility of its business model. Through good fortune rather than good management, the business was not decimated. Significant investment has been made into the digital platform, and an omnichannel now exists for customers. Rob is confident this will both enhance customer relationships and strengthen the business model.

Raymond O'Flaherty, CEO of Metro Trains Melbourne (MTM), recognises that the organisation must determine if the business model is financially sustainable. Its immediate challenge is to identify what changes are needed to ensure it can continue to be a stable organisation that is a great place to work and serves the needs of commuter travel patterns throughout Melbourne every day. Moving beyond the pandemic, at least for the foreseeable future, commuter confidence will require train services that are less crowded, cleaner, more comfortable, and safer. In short, the pre-COVID-19 model won't work. Workplace flexibility is here to stay. For an organisation such as MTM that requires many frontline roles, determining how flexibility works throughout the organisation will be an ongoing focus.

The pandemic has reduced the visibility of senior leaders as it has been more challenging to be onsite with staff due to COVID-19 protocols. Raymond is eager to return to the pre-pandemic practices of regularly engaging proactively and face to face with colleagues across every part of the organisation. It is vital to engage and listen to employees to build engagement and evolve a strong positive culture. The improved communication with employees via live streams and other channels is a lesson that will continue, as will be the increased focus on mental health and resilience. This isn't to say these topics weren't crucial before the pandemic. Instead, their importance has been heightened since February 2020, and MTM recognises the significance of continuing to provide better services for staff in these areas moving forward.

Raymond emphasises that staff and commuter health and safety will continue to be a priority. Maintaining practices to minimise the spread of COVID-19 remains a central focus and will be crucial for the process of moving beyond the lockdowns associated with the pandemic. Overall, the lessons from the past two years will enable MTM to operate better for its employees, the commuting public of Melbourne, and its other key stakeholders.

Sue Hayter is a multi-award-winning mortgage broker mentor and founder of Quality Financial Group & Trusted Mortgage Broker. The shift to flexible working has enabled clients to interact with mortgage brokers from a "whole person" perspective. Sue explains that the usual sounds of household living, pets and young children walking into view on the screen, even if blurred by artificial backgrounds, have become acceptable during the pandemic. This acceptance has led to endearingly different conversations where brokers and their clients have shared stories about their pets, home-schooling challenges, and more. This shift is a positive for the industry as it enhances the broker-client relationship. An unexpected benefit of meeting online is that it reduces the risk to brokers of visiting a home where their safety may be at risk. While such issues were rare, meeting online has effectively eliminated this challenge which is a positive for broker safety.

Sue has noticed that single people have worked when they otherwise would have been commuting, creating productivity benefits. Parents with school-aged children have worked on and off over an extended period throughout the day and evening and are, in many cases, exhausted. Sue is interested in seeing whether single people's productivity remains the same when some return to the office and lose the "extra" time they had gained from not commuting. In contrast, the return to school for children will be a welcome relief for parents.

While the pivot to signing online documents has been excellent (for example, the digitalisation of systems and processes has produced automatic face recognition software to eliminate identity fraud), ensuring online data is secure will be an ongoing challenge for the industry that has already seen significant growth in the number of lenders in the market. Due to a range of issues associated with how client income has been affected throughout the pandemic, more people are seeking the expertise of a broker to assist them with obtaining finance. As a result, the mortgage broker industry is growing. Responding to the growth and moving online, lenders have improved their communication and education with brokers through the significantly enhanced online learning opportunities and sessions available for brokers to attend. Sue believes these shifts are here to stay.

A challenge that remains unresolved relates to an issue that isn't specific to mortgage brokers but affects anyone who requires online data and document security. SMS and email scams have exploded throughout the pandemic. Each erodes the confidence of the general public in transacting online. If left unchecked, there will likely be a tipping point where many industries will be negatively affected. Moving forward, it will be in everyone's interests for governments and law enforcement agencies to eradicate this fraudulent behaviour.

Kristina Hermanson, managing director of FMC Australia – New Zealand (FMC ANZ), agrees with all previous leaders and believes that flexible work is here to stay. Throughout the second half of 2020 and up until the Sydney lockdown in May 2021, Kristina's Sydney-based office trialled a model intending to sustain the company's culture while offering continued flexibility for staff. Working from home for new staff poses a specific challenge that Kristina believes creates difficulties in nurturing a company's culture. For the trial, all staff worked in the office on Tuesdays and Wednesdays, and individual teams collaborated to choose one other day per week to attend the office. Team members worked from home on the other two days of the week. Due to the trial's success, Kristina is confident this model will continue when restrictions allow a return to the office. Of course, the world is constantly changing, so Kristina remains open to working with staff should the model prove unproductive.

The blurred line between work and parenting is now clear for all to see due to the pandemic. Kristina, herself a working mother, believes employers will benefit from remaining compassionate toward parents and continuing to innovate effective ways to support working parents as we move into 2022 and beyond. In addition, six team members have been recruited from the Australian team to roles within FMC Global. One of those team members has relocated to Singapore, and another is remaining in Wagga Wagga until it is safe also to move to Singapore, while the other four remain in Australia. Kristina believes this is an indication of the truly global nature of the workforce and will be an outcome of the pandemic that will gather speed over the coming years. While the opportunity to relocate for these staff will probably occur in the future, the requirement to migrate to continue in the roles is less likely. More staff will continue to work remotely across time zones, creating a more competitive environment for talent.

Kristina believes in "inclusive leadership," a form of leadership described by Bernadette Dillon and Julia Bourke from Deloitte. Creating and increasing trust with employees will be core to organisational success as we move beyond the pandemic. Leaders will need to be increasingly vulnerable to their team members as flexible work arrangements and uncertainty remain. The deliberate nurturing of an inclusive company culture will be essential, as will be the opportunities to support the culture through in-person and digital platforms. An inclusive culture is suitable for the people in the organisation, but it is also great for business. The diversity in global markets and the burgeoning middle class throughout Asia, India and Africa, demand that organisations have the capacity to innovate throughout their entire value chain. And innovation is catalysed by diversity. FMC ANZ has nearly doubled in size over the past five years. The deliberate creation of an inclusive culture provides the resilience and innovation required to sustain droughts, floods, trade wars, volatility and now a pandemic.

However, inclusive leadership can only occur if it is genuine. If you believe people are resources and want to become an inclusive leader because you read the business case and thought you ought to "jump on board," it won't work. It would be best to believe in inclusive leadership first, emphasised by its six traits: cognizance, curiosity, cultural intelligence, collaboration, commitment, and courage. This lesson is essential for leaders who intend to learn their way forward out of the pandemic and beyond.

Like Rob Clayton, Kristina is eager to get out and see the staff in the field and FMC ANZ's customers throughout Australia and New Zealand. As a confessed hugger, Kristina would love to wrap her arms around them and can't wait for it to be safe to do so! In-person connection is the element of her role she misses the most and is keen to eyeball staff and customers to check on how they have coped during the period she and her team have been unable to leave Sydney.

The education sector has experienced a disruption like no other. In January 2020, educators would have never believed they would spend the best part of the next two years teaching students remotely. Frank Catalano, principal at Glen Waverley Primary School, believes that education will never be the same. Despite the challenges of remote learning, many lessons from the experience will positively impact education beyond the pandemic. Pedagogy has become more transparent, the collaboration between teachers within and across schools has increased, and resistance to technology has effectively disappeared. Awareness of different learning styles and how to adapt and innovate to meet the needs of students and the critical importance of the connection between teachers and students have surfaced as essential for effective learning. For some students, remote education has improved their academic performance due to increased student agency and specialised support.

The awareness of mental health and well-being has risen dramatically, including understanding the different range of challenges staff have experienced depending on their situation at home. People living alone have had challenges, as have people living with large families and everyone in-between. Parents and teachers have "normalised" asking for help, which is a positive Frank hopes lasts beyond the pandemic.

Students have yearned for attention from their teachers. The crucial roles that playing and socialising contribute to a holistic approach to education are now understood throughout the broader community. Screen-free time and the value of family time spent doing some of the simpler things in life, such as going for walks and cooking and eating meals together, have been evident. Parents have a far greater appreciation of the work teachers do, especially for younger children. Frank believes this increased awareness has raised the community's view of the teaching profession, attracting more people to consider it a worthwhile career. Parent-teacher interviews can be extended to include other family members such as grandparents and other carers. They can also be recorded when permission is provided for sharing with other relevant people. Schools will be equipped to cater for students who may have extended stays away from school due to health issues and hospitalisation. Students moving schools may join their new school online before physically attending the school later in the year.

Many questions remain unanswered for educators. What will be the residual effect on teachers? Will some leave the profession due to having been burned out over the past two years? There is also an enormous impact on the importance of attracting staff that are open-minded to teaching in different paradigms. As schools have learned how to pivot between on-site and remote learning, will a similar form of learning be required to adapt to unknown challenges that will surface because of returning to school? What long-term effect will lockdowns have on the development of children's social skills? School leaders must remain agile and open-minded about meeting these challenges as children return to on-site learning. As they have done throughout the pandemic, entire school communities will need to continue to work together to overcome these issues.

It is now over to you. Take action. Remember, you are leading human beings, not human resources. Leading engaged employees is better for you, better for them and better for productivity. Be aware of your mental models and deliberately create the opportunity for shared ones to be developed throughout your teams and organisation. Understand how the evolution of the human brain affects our behaviour, take deliberate action to connect and empathise with the people you lead, and ensure role clarity exists for all people. You can never underestimate the power of vision. How alive, relevant, and shared is your vision? Does it exist? If you need to, start the process, and re-vitalise your vision to be relevant to the people you lead.

Develop the conversational skills that underpin everything this book recommends. Developing these skills will require effort, action, and plenty of smart, hard work. I encourage you to have the courage to include open, honest feedback as an essential element of the culture you deliberately choose to create for your organisation. Please recall that you either get the culture you choose to make, or you get the culture you get. Which version do you believe will equip you better to lead as you emerge from the disruption caused by the pandemic?

Please contact me via **www.disruptionleadershipmatters. com/contact** and let me know if the book has inspired you to change your practices. Little things matter, so if you start by changing the titles of your HR staff, please share the new names you have chosen. Let me know what behaviours the book has reinforced for you and what is new for you. Finally, if you have stories about leadership that is great for the leaders, followers, and your organisation, please send them to me. A new edition is only as far away as an updated set of stories.

Acknowledgements

Writing a book such as this one cannot be completed alone. Many people have assisted in various ways, from support to proofreads, contributions, interviews, suggestions, and more. Firstly, I want to thank my wife, Michelle. This year we celebrate 25 years of marriage. Her love, support and advice and unwavering belief in what I do through the business provide me with energy, especially in the downtimes (yes, folks, I experience them, too). Our five children, Liam, Sienna, Callum, Aiden, and Darcy, inspire me to be the best I can be every day. Each of them has had their unique experience of the pandemic, and each of them has been truly amazing. They have continued to accept responsibility for their learning throughout the most challenging time in all our lives. Mum and I could not be prouder of each of you!

To Maree Harris. Your engagement with the idea for the book and ongoing encouragement and conversations inspired me to keep going. I am forever in your debt. Thank you to Nicky McKeown, who completed an early edit of the book's first section and Marcus Pitt for your proofread and suggestions for the final chapter.

Thank you to Raymond O'Flaherty, Rob Clayton, Kristina Hermanson, Sue Hayter, Frank Catalano, Tim Lee, Lyn Nye,

Graeme Cowan, Rebecca Staines, Gareth Kent, Norman Same, Shelly McElroy, David Allt-Graham, Mike Stasiuk, Mario Stanisic, Daniel Auld, Michael Lewis and Ben Kenyon. Your timely responses never ceased to amaze me, despite your hectic schedules. To Lawrence Cupido, Caitlyn Dunne, Andrew Buxton, Stuart Major, Brett Cox, Hannah Jensen, Neil Walsh, Joy Gao, Joelene Schembri, Pat Henderson, Sandra Marinacci-Orbach, Joe Van Roosmalen, Sam Kane, Matt D'Orazio, Stefano Bianchi, Megan Capicchiano, Julia Dwyer, Jason Craig, and Pat McGlenchy, thank you for your willingness for your stories to be shared within these pages or for providing suggestions for improvements to the manuscript.

Thank you to Andrew Cole, Allan Preiss, Ian Berry, Zixi Liang and Zara Kattan for your suggestions for people and topics to include in the book.

To William and Irina Webster and your team from the Australian Self-Publishers Group, thank you. Your experience and guidance are appreciated.

Thank you to all my clients over the past 15 years. I am forever grateful for your trust and loyalty from those of you who have continued to engage my services over many years. Thank you to the thousands of individuals I have had the honour to work with over the years. I have learned more from you than you realise. Please remain safe and healthy until we meet again.

Bibliography & Resources

Ackoff, R.L. (1999) *Re-Creating the Corporation – A Design of Organizations for the 21st Century.* Oxford University Press, Oxford.

Argyris, C., & Schon, D.A. (1996) *Organizational Learning II - Theory, Method, and Practice* Addison-Wesley, Massachusetts.

Bennis, W., Goleman, D., & O'Toole, J. (2008) *Transparency – How Leaders Create a Culture of Candor.* Jossey-Bass, San Francisco.

Bersin, J. (2016) "Why Diversity and Inclusion Has Become a Business Priority." Accessed 2nd August 2021 https://joshbersin.com/2015/12/why-diversity-and-inclusion-will-be-a-top-priority-for-2016/

Blanchard, K. & Ridge, G. (2009) *Helping People Win At Work – A Business Philosophy Called "Don't Mark My Paper Help Me Get An A."* Pearson Education, New Jersey.

Bourke, J. (2021) *Which Two Heads Are Better Than One?: The Extraordinary Power of Diversity of Thinking and Inclusive Leadership* 2nd Edition, Australian Institute of Company Directors, Sydney.

Brown, B. (2018) *Dare to Lead – Brave Work. Tough Conversations. Whole Hearts.* Ebury Publishing, London.

Callahan, C. (2016) *Putting Stories To Work – Mastering Business Storytelling.* Pepperberg Press, Melbourne.

Chapman, B. & Benguhe, C. (2021) "Bob Chapman Builds Colossal Success On Simple Premise: Treat People With Respect." https://www.ibtimes.com/bob-chapman-builds-colossal-success-simple-premise-treat-people-respect-3250401 15th July 2021

Chapman, B. & Sisodia, R. (2015) *Everybody Matters: The Extraordinary Power of Caring for Your People Like Family.* Penguin, USA.

Charvet, S.R. (2019) *Words That Change Minds – The 14 Patterns for Mastering the Language of Influence.* 3rd Edition. Institute For Influence, USA.

Cowan, G. (2021) "Episode #13 Spurred by tragedy to build a culture of care - Chris Murray, Managing Director, Energy Power Systems Australia." *The Caring CEO Podcast.* Accessed 3 July 2021. https://podcasts.apple.com/au/podcast/the-caring-ceo/id1555420803

Covey, S.R., (1989) *The 7 Habits of Highly Effective People.* Simon and Schuster, New York.

Dillon, B. & Bourke, J. (2016) *The Six Signature Traits of Inclusive Leadership - Thriving in a Diverse New World.* Deloitte University Press, USA.

Dweck, C. (2006) *Mindset – How You Can Fulfil Your Potential.* Random House, New York.

Edmondson, A. (2018) *The Fearless Organisation.* Harvard University, Wiley, Boston.

Ericcson, K.A. & Pool, R. (2016) *Peak – How All of Us Can Achieve Extraordinary Things.* Penguin Random House, UK.

Fritz, R. (1989) *The Path of Least Resistance – Learning to Become the Creative Force in Your Own Life.* Fawcett Books, Toronto.

George, B. (2003) *Authentic Leadership - Rediscovering the Secrets of Creating Lasting Value.* Jossey-Bass, San Francisco.

George, D.F. (2021) *Diversity and Inclusion in the Organizations - How to Promote Equality in the Workplace and Benefit From It.* Davide Pelagatti, USA.

Godin, S. (2011) *The Dip: A Little Book That Teaches You When to Quit (and When to Stick).* Little, Brown Book Group, London.

Harari, Y.V. (2011) *Sapiens: A Brief History of Humankind.* Vintage, London.

Hassed, C. & Chambers, R. (2016) *Mindfulness for Wellbeing and Peak Performance.* Free online course. Accessed 8 February 2016 https://www.futurelearn.com/courses/mindfulness-wellbeing-performance

Hock, D. (1999) *Birth of the Chaordic Age.* Berrett-Koehler Publishers, San Francisco.

Hofstede, G., Hofstede G.J. & Minkov, M. (2010) *Cultures and Organizations - Software Of The Mind - Intercultural Cooperation and Its Importance for Survival*. McGraw-Hill, New York.

Hunt, M. (1998) *Dream Makers - Putting Vision and Values To Work*. Davies Black Publishing, Palo Alto.

Kahneman, D. (2011) *Thinking, Fast and Slow*. Penguin Books, USA.

Mandela, N. (1994) *A Long Walk to Freedom*. Abacus Books, Great Britain.

McElroy, S. (2021) "The Little Things That Create Significant Change." Leading Teams. Accessed 25 July 2021. https://www.leadingteams.net.au/the-little-things-that-create-significant-change/

McLean, R. (2006) *Any Given Team - Improving Leadership And Team Performance*. Paul G. Conroy, North Melbourne.

Orr, M. (2019) *Lean Out - The Truth About Women, Power, and the Workplace*. Harper Collins, USA.

Peters, T. (2018) *The Excellence Dividend - Principles for Prospering in Turbulent Times from a Lifetime in Pursuit of Excellence*. Nicholas Brealey Publishing, UK.

Pfeffer, J. & Sutton, R.I (1995) *The Knowing-Doing Gap - How Smart Companies Turn Knowledge Into Action*. Harvard Business Review Press, New York.

Pink, D.H. (2009) *Drive - The Surprising Truth About What Motivates Us*. Riverhead Books, New York.

Ridge, G. (2021) *The Unexpected Learning Moment - Lessons in Leading a Thriving Culture Through Lockdown 2020*. Telemachus Press, Dublin, USA.

Rucci, A.J., P. Kirn, S.P.& T. Quinn, R.T. (1998) "The Employee-Customer-Profit Chain at Sears." *Harvard Business Review*. January–February, Boston.

Rutherford, A. (2019) *Neuroscience And Critical Thinking*. Kindle Publishing, USA.

Senge, P. (2006) *The Fifth Discipline - The Art & Practice of The Learning Organization*. Revised and Updated Edition. Random House, UK.

Sinek, S. (2019) *The Infinite Game*. Penguin Random House, USA.

Sinek, S. (2011). *Start With Why*. Penguin Random House, UK.

Volo, K. (2020) *Evoloshen Academy*. Member Interviews. www.evoloshen.com

Willink, J. & Babin, L. (2015) *Extreme Ownership - How U.S. Navy Seals Lead and Win*. St. Martin's Press, USA.

Willink, J. & Babin L. (2018) *The Dichotomy of Leadership*. St Martin's Press, USA.

About the Author

Gary Ryan is the founder of Organisations That Matter, a boutique consulting firm in Melbourne, Australia. Gary works with organisations in a wide range of industries, including public transport, agriculture, building services, finance, banking, federal, state, and local gov-ernment, universities, arboriculture, primary and secondary schools, pro-

fessional sport, and individual leaders who desire to improve their lives and the lives of the people they serve.

Gary is the ninth of 11 children and a twin. As such, he says teamwork has been part of his life ever since conception! He is happily married to Michelle, and together they have five chil-dren. With Michelle, nothing has been more critical for Gary than leading their family through this challenging period. Everything he and Michelle have learned throughout their lives has been placed under the microscope, having spent more than 260 days living under strict lockdown rules.

In the mid-1990s, Gary was introduced to Servant Leadership and the theory and practice of Organisational Learning. These theories are constantly evolving and have spawned Authentic Leadership and Inclusive Leadership. The theoretical foundation of these bodies of knowledge has continued to influence Gary in everything he does. Most importantly, Gary believes in closing the gap between theory and practice, which is the space in which he has chosen to work. He focuses on leaders because they have the most significant influence on the culture within an organisation.

As a contributor to his local community, Gary has performed many roles as a volunteer coach and sports coordinator for the various local sporting organisations his children have attended.

Collect your free resources here:

https://disruptionleadershipmatters.com/resources
Password: L3Ad3r

Connect with Gary Ryan here at:

Website: https://orgsthatmatter.com

LinkedIn: https://www.linkedin.com/in/garyryan1

Twitter: @garyryans

YouTube: https://www.youtube.com/channel/
UCULM3ORiQHJn6M9giK2s11A

www.ingramcontent.com/pod-product-compliance
Lightning Source LLC
Chambersburg PA
CBHW071015180726
48291CB00004B/1468